Paul

His Defenders

Book 1

By

Ronna M. Bacon

Psalm 32:7 You are my hiding place; You preserve me from trouble; You surround me with songs of deliverance.

NKJV

Table of Contents

Chapter 1
Chapter 2
Chapter 3
Chapter 4
Chapter 5
Chapter 6
Chapter 7
Chapter 8
Chapter 9
Chapter 10
Chapter 11
Chapter 12
Chapter 13
Chapter 14
Chapter 15
Chapter 16
Chapter 17
Chapter 18
Chapter 19
Chapter 20
Chapter 21
Chapter 22
Chapter 23
Chapter 24
Chapter 25
Chapter 26
Chapter 27
Chapter 28
Chapter 29
Chapter 30
Chapter 31

Chapter 32
Chapter 33
Chapter 34
Chapter 35
Chapter 36
Chapter 37
Chapter 38
Chapter 39
Chapter 40
Chapter 41
Chapter 42
Chapter 43
Chapter 44
Epilogue
Dear Readers

Walking quickly towards the building housing the bookstore that he favoured, Paul Abecrombie drew in a deep breath. The early spring held a hint of the rain that had fallen overnight, drawing up the smell of fresh growth from the ground and the surrounding shrubbery. He squinted at the bright sun that seemed to be doing its best to cause life to spring up everywhere at once.

He held the door open for a beautiful lady, about his own age, as they reached it at the same time. The sun turned its attention to her black hair, sparkling off of it and from the depths of the deep green eyes that she raised towards him as her thanks wafted to his ears.

Paul rubbed at his dark brown hair, his hazel eyes on the move as he searched the store around him. He could feel something off in there that day. He just didn't know what. Waiting in line being the lady to grab a free coffee, Paul thought back over the last week. Away from their town of Oak City for a week on a security assignment, Paul was ready for a few days of relaxation. It had been a tough assignment, the man who they were to protect fighting them every moment of each day.

Sensing something off about the building, Paul turned in a circle. His senses had alerted him that there was a problem in the area. He walked away, heading for the manager. They spoke before the manager nodded. He trusted Paul's assessment. He walked back to his office, Paul pacing at his side.

"Paul, what do you think?" David Adams rubbed at his neck. He knew that Paul would not have approached him with his concerns unless they were that strong.

"I don't know, David. Something is off. I can feel it. And that feeling has saved us more than once." Paul stared at the open door. "You have security around today?"

"Not today. You're thinking a search of the building?"

"I am. If we can do that first, then we call in help. If you want, I can search for you." Paul was away at David's nod, knowing that something was off. And he could not ignore that feeling.

Paul swiftly searched the building, his feeling getting increasingly stronger as he approached the second floor. This floor was used for storage for the building. He paused at the top of the stairs, his keen eyes moving around the floor. He walked forward, a frown on his face as he concentrated on his task. He paused once more in front of a door to a room where he knew that paper products were kept. With a hand on the knob, he stopped himself. *Lord, what are You telling me? Something is in there, isn't there? And I just can't open that door.*

Running for the stairs, Paul slid down them almost without his feet touching them. David was waiting for him.

"Paul? Did you find something?" David felt fear at the look on Paul's face.

"There's something wrong upstairs. The room where you store your paper products? Something's off there. I couldn't open it. I would suggest that we clear the store and call in the authorities. You may need to have the bomb squad go through." Paul watched David closely, seeing his face pale at the thought.

"A bomb?" David almost stuttered out the words. He spun, heading for the customers, simply stating that they needed to close.

Paul took the other side of the store, his calmness as he asked the customers to leave sending them away without too much concern. He paused, a frown on his face. Someone was still in there, he could feel that. And he needed to find that person. Paul searched further, heading for an alcove tucked away in the back corner of the store. This alcove held hand crafts for local artists, limited in nature, but still a popular place for customers to browse.

Payten Byrne stood there, studying the blown-glass art. There were new pieces that intrigued her. She had her earbuds in, her music on low enough that she could barely hear it, but it was enough to block most sounds. She jumped and gave a small scream before spinning. Her mouth opened to spit out angry words at the man who had grabbed at her arm before her mouth snapped closed.

Paul stared at her for a moment, surprised at the anger that flared.

"We need to leave." He waited for her to move, frowning himself. He reached to pull down one of her earbuds. "Did you hear me? The building is being evacuated and now!" His voice was rough and harsh with his worry and yes, anger at her refusal to move.

"Says who?" Payten dug in her heels and refused to move.

Feeling the danger growing with each second that passed, Paul simply grasped her hand and pulled her with him, heading for the back door and safety. He just prayed that they reach it in time. He had no desire to become part of the debris of the building if what he suspected was true, that a bomb of some kind was in that room.

Payten tugged at her hand, desperate to release it. She never allowed anyone to touch her like that. An experience in her college years had destroyed that for her.

"Stop! I'll let you go once we're outside. For now, we don't have time to do that. I don't know that I can trust you to come with me." Paul simply pulled her with him as he broke into a run, his hand out to slam against the door. The door flew open, letting in the bright sunlight. He tugged Payten with him harder as his feet picked up their pace.

Payten just decided to run with him, her free hand reaching to pull out her earbuds and tuck them into a jacket pocket. She had no idea why she had been pulled out as she had been, but once they stopped, she would be demanding answers. Only that opportunity never came.

The sudden blast behind them hit them hard in their backs, sending them flying forward. Paul reached for Payten, wrapping her into his arm, hitting the pavement hard. He took the full force of the fall, his body protesting at the force which dropped them to the ground. Payten screamed before silence reigned around them.

Onlookers stared in horror as the building seemed to disintegrate in front of them, dropping into a pile of bricks, wood, and insulation. Flames began to lick at the debris, causing even more fear among David. He had not seen Paul emerge from the building. Running frantically around the pile, he could hear the sounds of the sirens rising and falling as emergency personnel rushed to the scene. He slid to a stop, a hand across his forehead as he searched for Paul. A sound of dismay erupted from him as he saw the two bodies.

Please, Lord, let them be alive. And let it be Paul. I don't want to explain to Don what happened to one of his team members.

Dropping to his knees, David threw away debris that covered the couple. He reached with a shaking hand to search for pulses. His breath blew out in relief. Turning, he waved at the officer who ran towards him, a hand to his radio to call for help.

"What happened, David?" The officer knew David well. His head tilted as he recognized Payten. "Payten? She was here?"

"She was. So was Paul. Paul felt something off about the building, searched it, and then asked me to clear it until we could have the bomb squad come through. He felt something off, he said, on the second floor."

The officer stared at David and then down at Paul. He had not recognized Paul at first. He was on his feet, running for the police chief, who had shown up. He needed to be back there. Waving at paramedics, he simply pointed behind the building.

Chapter 2

Moving carefully but quickly, the paramedics assessed Paul and Payten, calling for the backboards and neck collars. Payten began to rouse, fighting somewhat to free herself until she realized that she was indeed hurt and indeed needed medical assistance. Her responses were quiet but pain filled. She didn't know what had happened to the man who had rushed her from the building, but she did need to find him at some point and thank him. She knew that she had not been very nice to him. Payten was moved away from the site as soon as she was ready, concern on the faces of the men and women working around the couple.

Toryn Knight, the police chief for Oak City, walked towards where the couple lay, still being worked on by the emergency teams. He frowned as he recognized Payten, a forensics technician from their force. He would speak with her, once she had been assessed. He also knew which detective he would ask for. Aidan McNeill would be his choice. Aidan had been on the force in Elmton as a patrol officer before jumping at the chance to take on the position of a detective in Oak City.

He frowned once more as he stared down at the man who by now had been shifted to the backboard. Paul? What was he doing here? He listened quietly as a patrol officer explained what David had told him.

"Paul searched the building?" Toryn's question was not unexpected. It was what he had come to expect from any member of Don's security team. Don was a good friend and fellow Christian.

"From what David said, he did. There was a room on the second floor that he was concerned about and asked David to clear the building until he could have someone come in and search it. David seemed to think that Paul was thinking a bomb."

Toryn nodded. He knew the specialties of each of Don's team and that weapons and bombs were Paul's. If Paul had suspected a bomb, then that was like what it had been.

"We'll have some work to sort through all that. I'll be at the hospital." Toryn walked away, his heart heavy for Payten. She had been through enough in her life, he decided, losing her parents in a house fire, being physically assaulted while at college, and now this.

Don walked through the door in the ambulance bay at the hospital, searching for Paul. He had been home, working around outside when he had been called. Paul had no family, losing his parents in a flash flood when he was young. He searched for the charge nurse, finding her and then heading for Paul.

Paul had not yet awakened, the blow from a brick knocking him unconscious. The nurses worked around him, nodding at Don as he waited for them to allow him to walk forward.

Able at last to approach the stretcher, Don's face tightened as he saw the cut on Paul's head, the blood darkening his hair. He was concerned but grateful for the care that Paul was receiving. He turned slightly as he heard footsteps approaching him in turn.

Doc Walters stood there. He was a fellow churchgoer but also a good friend to Don.

"Don? You're here?"

"I am, Doc. How is Paul?" Don was concerned. He knew that his team had a free week the following week but they were planning on training. He needed Paul there. Now, he wasn't sure if he would be physically fit to do that.

"Paul? He's taken a good blow to his head. He's battered by debris and from hitting the pavement himself. We've taken the imaging that we need. Nothing broken, thank God for that. Multiple bruises. Some cuts from the debris as you can see. We may need to keep him in for the night, but we'll reassess that if he awakens. He can't be on his own."

"No, he can't. He's welcome with any of us, although three of the guys are away for the weekend." Don blew out a breath, thinking through where he could send him. "I'll take him home with me. It's not the first time that we've had to do something like this." Don frowned for a moment. "Someone says something about a lady?"

"There was. The teams apparently found Paul with Payten. She was hurt as well but is awake and talking. We'll need to find somewhere for her to stay."

"And we will. My sister is staying with me for the next couple of weeks while her home is painted and refreshed from that flood we had. Payten would be welcome to come with us."

"Thanks, Don. How be we go and find her?" Doc walked away, leaving Don to study Paul before he walked away.

Don stood outside Payten's room for a moment, watching as Doc spoke with her. The head of the stretcher was raised so that he could see her clearly. He walked forward as Doc turned and waved him forward.

"Payten? You can't stay on your own. Not for tonight. We don't need to keep you overnight. Don here has volunteered to have you stay with him and his sister for overnight."

Payten's face was mutinous. She felt that she was well enough to stay on her own. She never liked staying with anyone else. Payten valued her privacy too much to do that.

"It's what it is, Payten. You either find someone on your own to stay with or you stay with Don. He has a security team, in case you didn't know that. The man who dragged you from the building? That's Paul, one of his team members, who pulled you from the building. I know you. You likely fought him on that, didn't you?"

Payten glared at him before her face turned sheepish.

"I did." Her voice held shame. "I didn't know him. And when he grabbed my hand, I panicked."

"I thought that. Now, Don is willing to help you out, at least for the overnight hours. Something has been going on with you for a long time, Payten. You need help with that. It's time to let it go."

Payten wiped at the sudden tears that overflowed before she gave a small nod. Doc was correct. She did need to let it go. Only, she didn't want to. *Lord, how do I do this? How do I let go of something that's I've buried so deep and for so long?*

Don waited patiently. He had learned long ago that sometimes it took a person realizing that they needed help before they accepted it. He watched the emotions flickering across her face before she nodded, accepting his help. Don stepped away, calling his sister, simply asking her for help.

Chapter 3

Paul roused as he felt a hand on his shoulder. He strained to recognize the voice before he nodded. Pain shot through his head as he squinted against the light and the pain.

"Paul? Can you stand up?" Don was worried about Paul, a hand resting on his friend's shoulder.

"I don't know, Don. What happened? Are we home?" Paul gradually sat up, swinging his legs over the side of the bed.

"We are home. You were in the bookstore this morning, discovered a bomb, and just made it out in time. You were hurt by flying debris."

"I was?" Paul didn't doubt his words. "I don't remember."

"No, I don't think that you will. I'm taking you to my place for overnight. You can't be on your own." Don reached for Paul's arm and helped him to the waiting wheelchair.

Paul sank into it gratefully. His eyes closed as he tried to control the pain and the nausea. He didn't see Don nod to Payten who had stood near the room door, waiting for Paul to respond to Don.

"Come on, Payten. We'll get you to my place. If you need to stop at yours, we can do that. Daci is expecting both you and Paul to stay overnight. It's fine. I have lots of room."

"That would be fine, Don. Thank you. I'm supposed to work tomorrow but I don't know that I can."

"Not likely. Call your supervisor. I'm sure by now that they're aware that you've been involved in this incident. Toryn was around."

"I thought so. He said that Aiden McNeill would be around to talk with us." Payten turned on the front seat of Don's truck to watch Paul. "He's hurting."

"He is. In many ways, Payten. Just like you." Don didn't know her history. He could just read people.

Payten shot him a glance before she nodded. Don was right. She was hurting in many ways. It was time for her to start healing. Only to start healing, she had to dig way down into herself, to the areas that she had buried deep over time. She had covered them as deep as she could. Payten knew that it would hurt to do that. She just prayed for God to send her a defender, someone to protect her and stand between her and whoever it was that wanted to harm her.

"I do, Don. I do. It's time. I just need to find someone who can help me." Payten stared out of the side window, a sober look on her face. She had no idea who to turn to despite having many friends on the police force. To some extent, she was ashamed of what had happened to her when she had suffered the physical assault.

"We'll help you, Payten." Paul's voice from the back seat stilled her motions of rubbing her hands on her jeans. "You're not alone in this. And never alone again." Paul made his choice, knowing that he would not walk away from her, not ever.

Don walked Payten to her front door, waiting as she unlocked it and turned off her security system. His hand stopped her in the entryway.

"Let me walk through your place first. Given what has happened, we need to be extra careful." Don walked through her house, finding it tidy and clean. "Okay, Payten. Grab what you need. And then we'll head for Paul's home to grab what he needs."

Payten nodded, scurrying away to pack a bag. She headed for her office area to grab her Bible and the book that she had been reading before she hesitated and grabbed her laptop and the charging cords for both her phone and the computer. Payten hesitated for a moment, knowing that Don was right. She needed to be with someone that night. She was just uncertain if Don's was the place to hide. And hiding was exactly what she felt as if she was doing.

Don walked quickly through Paul's home, packing a bag for him and grabbing what he would need for the next few days. He was determined that Paul did not stay on his own. He searched for the little calico cat that Paul had rescued, cradling her close before he found her carrier. He also reached for her food. Don had a tuxedo cat himself and knew that the cats would be fine together. They had spent many hours in one another's homes, searching for the other when they were alone.

Paul watched Don return with his burdens, reaching for the cat crate. His finger reached through the door, finding Kiva licking at it. A tiny mew came from her, protesting being locked up as she saw it.

Payten had shifted on her seat, watching Paul, a frown on her face. She had not expected him to have a cat. But then again, how would she have known that? She didn't know him, didn't know his likes and dislikes, and not likely ever would.

Don helped Paul into the house to the guest suite on the main floor. He steadied him on his feet for a moment, his eyes worried.

"Paul? You need to be lying down. Or do you want to clean up first?"

"I would like that last option, Don. I feel so grungy. Thank you." Paul headed for the ensuite, familiar enough with it as he had stayed with Don previously when they were working through assignments with their team. He simply thanked Don as he handed him his bag.

Payten stood in the living room, arms wrapped around herself. She was not sure where she was to be. Don had simply pointed towards the kitchen as he helped Paul. Payten didn't know him well enough to head there without his presence. She jumped as she felt a paw tapping at her knee. A beautiful tuxedo cat stood there, meowing at her. She reached for the cat, her head whirling for a moment as she bent over.

Don laughed as he approached her, knowing that his cat had made a new friend.

"Kira's found you, I see." Don continued to laugh as he headed for the kitchen, reaching to pick up Kiva. "She usually hides from visitors."

"She does?" Payten followed him, pulling back a chair to sit as he pointed at it. "So, why hasn't she?"

"She's sensitive. She knows if someone is hurting and tries hard to make it all better." Don turned on the coffee pot. "Paul may be out for something to drink and eat. On the other hand, he may just crash. You're about ready to do that as well."

Payten sighed, knowing that Don was correct.

"I need to have something to eat, if you don't mind, Don. I'm feeling a little shaky."

"Not a problem." He looked around as he heard the back door open and close. "Daci? I wondered where you were?"

"I needed to pick up a few more things from the grocery store. I also stopped by my place. It's coming along so well. The painter told me that they're working as they can around other jobs." Daci sent her bags on the counter, walking into her brother's hug. "I told them that was not a problem. I had a roof over my head, unlike others who needed their work more. It's what Christ would have done."

"It is, sis. It is. Now, this is Payten Byrne. She's here for overnight at least." Don watched as Daci simply swept Payten into a hug. That was what his younger sister did.

"Payten? That is such a beautiful name. Spell it for me." Daci sat beside Payten, taking with thanks the mug of coffee that Don handed her. "You are indeed very welcome here. And if you don't want to be on your own when you go home, I'll just go with you. If my house was finished, I'd just take you there."

Payten stared at her, feeling her heart beginning to break free from the bonds that had held it for so long. She was unable to speak for the tears that clogged her throat.

Chapter 4

The next morning, Paul roused, on his feet and dressed, not recognizing the room for a moment. He felt something around his feet and found Kiva there. Reaching down to pick her up, he cradled her close. Her little pink tongue came out to lick at his finger before he headed for the kitchen. Finding the coffee already perked, Paul reached to pour a cup and then turned. He could hear conversation from Don's office and headed that way.

Don looked up as he heard Paul and waved him into the room, pointing to a chair. Paul sat, his mug of coffee on the desk, his hand stroking Kiv]==a's fur, hearing her purring.

Setting aside his phone, Don studied his friend, seeing that Paul's eyes were brighter although he was still in pain.

"How are you this morning, Paul?" Don waited patiently for Paul to respond.

"About like that. The headache is better. I just don't feel that great."

"No, you're not going to. You'll be hurting for a while. So will Payten."

"Payten? Where is she?" Paul set Kiva down, his hands on the chair arms to push himself upright.

"She's in the sunroom with Daci. We'll let them talk for a bit. Daci's getting Payten to open up some. I don't want to intrude."

Paul relaxed once more, his eyes on Don.

"Do we have any information on what happened? I'm still fuzzy about it."

"You thought that you had found a bomb on the second floor of the building. You had the store cleared and found Payten. The two of you were running from the building when it exploded. You were thrown down and hit with flying debris. Do you remember anything?"

Paul shook his head, regretting it. He didn't remember anything from the day before.

"I don't remember anything from yesterday." Paul's eyes slid closed as he tried hard to remember. He shook his head. "Not a thing comes to mind. I know that I gave my statement, not that there was much to give."

"That's what Toryn said. He's assigning Aidan to the investigation." Don sat back himself, a frown on his face. "It doesn't make sense, Paul. Why bomb the bookstore? What did David have there that someone wanted to destroy?"

"I have no idea. We would need to talk with him." Paul paled as he had a horrible thought. "What if someone had followed me yesterday and set the bomb, knowing that I was there? Is that even possible?"

"It is." Aidan McNeill spoke from the doorway before he walked in and sat in a chair next to Paul. "What can you tell me about who might be after you?"

Paul and Don shared a look. They would need to go back through their cases and that would take time.

"I have no idea, Aidan." Paul shook his head, finding the headache returning.

"I need you to work through that." He looked around as he heard footsteps approaching them. "Payten? What can you tell me?" He was on his feet, seeing the distressed look on her face. "Payten? We're friends, but I'm here as the investigator. You need to talk with me."

Payten shook with the force of her emotions. Daci's arm was around her, distress on her face. She watched as Paul approached Payten, reaching out to hug her. Aidan was surprised as Payten allowed this, knowing that she refused physical contact with anyone.

"Payten? We need you to speak with us." Paul drew her further into the room and down to the loveseat that Don had in there. "Talk to me. Tell me what is wrong. I can tell that something is."

Payten nodded, unable to speak for a moment, her emotions in a whirl. She knew that she needed help to investigate what had been troubling her and find out who had been following her all these years. That was obvious.

"There is. I just don't know where to start." Payten felt Paul's arm around her. She felt safe and secure for once in her adult life. She had been so young when her parents had died that she had not had that for years. She also felt that Paul would defend her against whoever it was.

Payten's head turned slightly as she studied Paul beside her. His face had bruising and cuts and scrapes, but his character showed through.

"I can, I guess. It's not a pretty story." Payten stopped speaking once more, her hand covering her mouth.

"It never is, Payten. We all know that. Don and I? We have a security team and have seen and heard horrible things that have been done to others. Daci? She's a resource counsellor for a woman's shelter. She's seen horrible things as well."

"You are? She has? And Aidan has seen it all as well." Payten's head dropped as she prayed. She needed the courage that only God would provide to her for her to speak. She just wasn't sure if she was ready.

Don simply began to pray for Payten, for a release of what she had kept hidden for so many years. He prayed for peace for her, for healing, and for resolve and strength to go forward. They all felt the presence of God in the room, knowing that He was indeed there.

Payten raised her head, determination on her face. It was time, she knew. It was time to face her nemesis and defeat whoever it was.

"Aidan, you are aware that I am an orphan. My parents died in a house fire. It was deemed to be arson. The smoke detectors didn't go off so they could be warned.   They   had   been   tampered   with,   the

---

investigator discovered. I had been away on a school trip with my grade nine class. When I got back to the school, the authorities were waiting for me. I ended up in foster care as there was no one to take me in. It was hard. I managed to get a number of scholarships and with the money from the insurance that my parents had taken out, I entered college." She halted her words, not sure if she could even continue.

Paul's arm tightened around her, feeling her leaning harder against him. He continued to pray for her. He knew what it was like to lose parents at a young age and grow up in foster care.

Aidan looked up from his notes. He had done some preliminary work on Payten that morning and had been shocked by what he had found. He needed to talk with her about that. He just wasn't sure that she would be willing to do that in front of the others.

Chapter 5

Drawing in a shuddering breath, Payten refused to look up at those in the room with her. She just felt that they would condemn her. Aidan would not, she knew. His character was such that he would not condemn her. Instead, he would search for anything and everything that would help her.

Paul tilted his head to watch her face, seeing the distress on her face. He did not know her and, therefore, did not know what she had faced in the past. All he knew is the lady that he was holding to comfort her was in distress, needed his help, and drew from him his prayers for her.

Payten kept her eyes down, not wanting to see the censure on their faces. She drew in a deep shuddering breath, real to talk but not sure where to begin.

"I don't know where to begin. When I was at college, I was physically assaulted. I had a broken humerus on my left arm, a dislocated shoulder, and three broken fingers on that hand. That was from the strong grip that my assailant had on my hand. He dragged me across a parking lot and slammed me against a car. He also beat me, leaving me in a broken heap on the ground. Someone saw him and ran towards us, chasing him away. He stayed with me until help arrived. Since then, I have had a fear of footsteps on pavement. I don't handle physical contact very well. And yes, I have had counselling for it."

———

There were shocked looks of horror on their faces. Aidan nodded, knowing that Payten had described what he had discovered. He had found that investigation but had hesitated to ask her about it. Paul's arms tightened around her, finding her moving closer to him without even thinking about it.

Daci watched her before sharing a look with Don. What Payten had said was a common thread to what she was told at the woman's shelter. It distressed her that a new friend had gone through that.

"They have not found the man responsible?" Don reached for a pad of paper and a pen, making notes from what she had said.

"No, there wasn't enough information to do so. At the time, they did not have security cameras focused on the parking lots. That changed after my assault." Payten drew in a deep breath, feeling free for the first time in years. "Thank you for listening. I know that I needed to talk about it. I just couldn't."

"It took the shock from what we went through to free you from that. We will look into this for you. We also have a friend who will, with your permission." Paul prayed for his new friends, knowing that he would be reaching out to his friend in Riverville, a lady who could find information that no one else could.

Payten turned her head to Paul, disconcerted for a moment to find him so close. She never let anyone this close. But something about her told her that he was the one who would help her to end this. She needed that defender so desperately. Had God really

---

provided someone just for her? It would be an answer to her prayer if He had.

Don hesitated for a moment, his eyes on Paul. Paul's eyes locked with his before Paul nodded. They had to help her. It was not in them to walk away if someone needed their help. And Payten really needed their help. Don frowned for a moment, seeing the interest in Payten that Paul was not yet ready to show. Knowing Paul so well, Don knew that Paul would not walk away from her, even if it meant harm to himself. That was how they all were.

Daci began to pray for her new friend, bringing her to the throne of grace, pleading with God for relief for Payten, a freeing from the fear that held her in its strong grip and had for so many years.

"What do we do for you, Payten? We want to help you, but we'll need you to work with us." Paul patiently waited for her to speak, knowing from experience that it might take a while.

Payten nodded, pushing at his arms to rise and walk away. Daci was on her feet, following her. She knew that sometimes victims needed time to confront their fear when it came out. She would be there for her and help her in any way that she could. Her prayer for her new friend petitioned God for peace for her and for someone to defend Payten.

Paul leaned forward, rubbing at his temples. His headache had worsened. He was on his feet, heading for his bedroom to seek medications to relieve it. Instead, Paul paused at the door to the sunroom, standing beside Daci.

"Has she said anything?" Paul kept his voice low.

"No, she hasn't. And she not likely will for a while. Or she might not say anything at all. It's how it goes. If she decides not to say anything, I'm not sure how we'll get her to talk."

Paul nodded at that. He knew from experience that was the case. He observed Payten as she heard them and turned to confront them. He shook his head, walking away from the doorway. Now was not the time for a confrontation.

Payten moved to stand in the doorway, watching Paul disappear into the bedroom.

"Did he just do that?" Payten was surprised.

"He does. He'll walk away until you're ready to talk for as long as it takes you. Any of Don's team will do that." Daci wrapped an arm around Payten. "I know what you do for a living, Payten. Are you back to work tomorrow?"

"I am. I just don't know if that's safe for my fellow workers." Payten didn't want to go home. She had felt someone around her home. She just hadn't seen anyone on the security cameras that she had set up. "And I don't feel safe at home."

Aidan had appeared just outside the doorway as had Paul and Don. The three men shared a look. This was more important, they decided among themselves, than going to church that morning. It would not be the first time that they had missed a service for a friend.

—

Paul moved towards Payten, finding her with her eyes on him, not moving backwards from him. He could sense the fear that she was trying hard to hide. That disturbed him greatly.

"Payten? Will you let us go over your home and outside it? Just to see where we need to up the security for it? And I would like to bring in a team member of Don's and mine. While we are all great with security, Mark is our expert." He waited patiently for her to digest his words and then to nod.

"That would be fine. When did you want to do that?"

"This morning. Mark's already on his way here, just to see how Paul is." Don dropped an arm across his sister's shoulders. "And if I know Daci, she'll want to move in with you for the next couple of weeks, if that is what you want."

Payten blinked rapidly against the tears that just had to appear in her eyes. She felt wanted and loved by these new friends. How could she say no? She simply nodded before Paul reached for her hands to pray for just her.

Chapter 6

Mark Monaghan walked towards Payten's home. He had re-routed there when Paul called him, simply asking him to check out the security on a friend's home. He had been puzzled at the text that he had received. This was not Paul to ask for help for a new friend and a lady at that. He had called Don, asking if this was indeed the case. Don had simply agreed after telling Mark what had happened to Paul on the day before.

His eyes assessed Payten's home, liking the bungalow. It was small but neat and tidy. He nodded to himself before he frowned as he saw Paul walking towards him.

"Paul? What did you go and do?" Mark stopped walking, assessing Paul's slow walk. "You're hurting."

"I am. It's not what I planned. You've spoken with Don."

"I have. Did you really have to go and do that?" Mark grinned for a moment before he sobered.

"I certainly didn't plan it. I had to get Payten out of there."

"Payten?" Mark knew a lady named Payten from church. He had been introduced to her a few months previously at a dinner. "Does she work for the police force?"

"She does. She's a forensics tech. Why? Do you know her?" Paul squinted at Mark, his headache pounding.

"I think so. I met her at a dinner a few months ago. Come on, pal. Let's get you to your lady and see what we can do to keep her safe." Mark walked away at that, leaving Paul staring after him.

My lady? What did Mark mean by saying that? I don't have a lady. Paul moved after Mark, not as rapidly as he would have liked.

Payten was waiting for him, a frown on her face as she watched Mark as he walked around her house. She could see the concentration on his face as he did so. She jumped slightly as she felt a hand take hers. Payten stared at her hand, seeing Paul's hand grasping hers.

Paul patiently waited for Payten. He would let her do what she needed to do, he knew. She needed to be in charge of what she did, taking her life back from the fear that had driven it for so long.

"Paul? Who is this?" Payten pointed towards Mark. She thought that he looked familiar. She just wasn't sure.

"That's Mark. He's one of my team mates. Right now? He's assessing the outside of your home and the property to see what you need to have installed to keep safe." His eyes met Don who stood nearby. "Then, he'll want to go through your home to assess the inside."

"That's fine." Payten rubbed at her cheek. "I don't like this. I feel uncomfortable at that."

"I'm sure that you do. For now, we'll try not to be too intrusive. Can you work with us on that?" Once more, Paul waited for Payten to respond.

Payten finally nodded, turning back towards her house. Paul didn't release her hand, simply walking with her. Daci watched from just inside the door, a question on her face. This was not Paul. He, like every man on Don's team, treated ladies with care and compassion, not overstepping any boundaries with them.

Payten spoke quietly with Mark as they stood in the kitchen. Paul had moved away with Don, walking outside to do their own assessment. Mark would confer with them when he had spoken with Payten.

"The other fellows are concerned about you, you know." Don watched Paul closely. The six men were all close in age in their late twenties and early thirties. They worked together as a team and had done so for a number of years.

"I thought that they would be. They've sent text messages. I gather that we are meeting tomorrow?"

"We are. We need to, Paul. We need to figure out what is going on with Payten and why that bomb was set. Who was the target?" Don was puzzled by that.

"I know, Don. It doesn't make sense. Was it placed after Payten and I entered the shop. I talked with David yesterday. He had security cameras in place but they were destroyed. The feed from an hour before the bomb exploded was down."

"Someone hacked into it." Don looked around, seeing Mark walking towards them. "Mark? David had mentioned to Paul that the security feed was down."

"It was. I spent yesterday evening with him, trying to recover it. We can't. Whoever hacked into it totally destroyed the feed."

"They did? Okay. Does Aidan know that?" Don was concerned about that.

"He does. I spoke with him from David's. He'll try and see whether one of their techs can recover it, but he said that if I couldn't recover it, it was unlikely that they could. I asked someone to try tracking back the hacker."

Don nodded once more. He knew his team would be investigating what and where they could be. If one of their team was hurt, they all were.

"Thanks, Mark." Paul turned to face the house, finding Payten walking rapidly towards him, Daci at her side.

Payten needed to be with Paul. She had never felt that way before. Paul made her feel safe and protected. His very being told her that he would defend her to the best of his abilities and that his friends would stand shoulder to shoulder with him.

Daci's gaze shifted between Paul and Payten. His concern for Payten was loud and clear to all who knew him. Don's men were quiet about their feelings, hiding them to some degree. They had to, given their line of work. Daci knew them, had spoken with them on many occasions, and treated them as if they were brothers to her.

Payten's hand tightened its grip on Paul's. She had no idea what to expect in the next few days. She was just grateful and thankful that God had provided someone to walk with her, many someones in fact.

Paul patiently waited once more. It was in his nature not to rush anyone. Instead, he would let whoever he was with determine the time that was taken, unless and only unless they were in danger.

Chapter 7

By the end of that week, Payten had grown accustomed to Paul either calling her or finding her at some point during the day. She had searched for him wherever she went, not knowing whether he would just show up. On a couple of days, she had found him sitting on the steps to her porch, a grin on his face, as she arrived home from work.

Paul, in turn, was working hard to determine who was after Payten. He didn't think someone was after him but that was not a hard fact. The team members had discussed the bombing and the fact about how odd it had been. David didn't seem to have any enemies.

Don watched Paul closely, assessing him as to his fitness for work. They were due out on an assignment during the following week for two days and then training on their own for the rest of the week. That was a necessary part of the team, their training to stay up to date on their skills.

Payten paused that Friday night, her eyes on her home. Paul was not there, and she missed him. She reached for her phone, scrolling through her messages. A smile crossed her face as she read the text messages from Don's team. Each one of the men had reached out to her over the week, introducing themselves and asking what they could do for her. Spinning as she heard footsteps approaching behind her, Payten stared at Daci.

"Daci? What are you doing here?" Her voice was almost a squeak, the fear in her doing that.

—

Daci grinned at her. She had just decided that Payten needed a friend with her that day. Paul, she knew, was out of town overnight on a prearranged trip. He had fretted that Payten would be on her own.

"I'm here to spend some time with a friend. Are you up for a guest for the weekend?" Daci held up a bag. "I hope that you are."

Payten drew in a deep breath. Daci was just who she needed that day.

"I am. Thank you. Where's Paul? I thought that he would be here." Payten unlocked her door and walked into the entryway, and stopped. "Something's off, Daci."

Daci's hand reached for her, pulling her backwards and then to her car. Her phone was out as she called for help from the authorities before she called Don.

"Don? Something's off at Payten's. We stepped inside and she could go no further than a few feet inside." She listened carefully before she responded. "I have called it in. Right now, she's at my car where I'm parked on the street. Okay. We'll see you in a bit."

Payten stared at her home, her fear drowning more and more.

"What's wrong with my home, Daci? Why couldn't I move forward?" Payten's arms wrapped around herself.

"Because God stopped you. He does that sometimes. It's like He puts a wall up in front of you.

Don and his team had have mentioned it many times." Daci wrapped an arm around Payten as a patrol officer approached her.

"Payten? Something wrong in your home?" Ted was a favourite of the crime lab, helping them as they needed help if they were on crime scenes.

"I don't know. After last week, I may just be too cautious. Something feels off. The security system has been upgraded just this week. I haven't pulled the feed yet. I should."

"In a moment. Let some of us walk through the house. Then, I'll come and find you."

Ted walked away and headed for the house, two other officers with him. Two others walked around the house, searching diligently for anything that should not be there.

Don hesitated before he approached Payten, Mark walking beside him. The other three team members, Thomas, Caleb, and Joshua, surrounded the two women, standing with their backs to them, their eyes searching that area.

Simply standing beside Payten, Don did not speak. He watched the activity around the house and the officers entering and exiting it.

Daci's eyes met Mark's eyes and the man nodded. They had expected something such as this to happen. It has just happened sooner than expected. Mark had reached out to Paul, who had not been surprised either. He just regretted that he was out of town until the next day, but the conference that he was attending could not be avoided.

Aidan walked through Payten's house, disturbed at the fact that her home had been invaded as it had been. He read the warning spray painted on her living room wall. Someone was after his friend, and he wanted that person who was responsible and wanted them right then.

"Ted? This is all?"

"It's not. The warning is also on the wall in her bedroom and the spare room. Her office is tossed, with the computer broken." Ted was angry that this damage had been done to a friend.

"Okay. Let's walk through this. The team is here and working?"

"They are. As soon as they heard it was Payten's home, they headed here as soon as they were free." Ted stood in the hallway, watching the activity in the office. "I just don't understand why Payten."

"None of us do." Aidan made his own search and investigation of the house, his phone out taking his own photos. Tucking his notepad away, he turned to the crime scene team. "How long will you be? Payten will want to walk through her home?"

"Maybe thirty minutes, Aidan." The lead tech looked up for a moment. "Then, you can walk her through it."

"Thanks." Aidan walked out of the back door, finding Ted waiting for him. "Ted? Anything out here?"

'The back door was broken in. That's how they got inside. The security system is down. I've asked one of the techs to look into it. I'm not sure that we'll find much."

"I don't know that we will. Thanks, Ted." Aidan walked the backyard, watchful for anything that was out of place. He had been there a number of times with some of their mutual friends. He didn't see anything overtly out of place but only Payten could tell them that.

Payten waited patiently, knowing the steps that were needed. The vibrating of her phone reached through to her at last. She reached for it, ready to delete the message. Only it was from Paul, just stating that he was praying for her and did she have someone with her. She smiled sadly as she responded that Daci and his team were there.

Paul set his phone down, a sad smile on his own face. It was good that his team was there. He wanted to be but couldn't leave. *God, please protect Payten. Help her to have peace in this situation. Help her to feel Your touch this night.*

———

Chapter 8

Staring in dismay at her home once she was allowed back inside, Payten fought back tears. She had no idea how she was going to cope. It just was too much. Don had been nearby and just swept her into a hug, doing for her what he would have done for Daci. Payten tears wet his shirt before she shoved back from him. Moving away, her hands wiped at her cheeks, knowing that she needed to paint the walls. She just didn't have the energy or stamina for that on that Friday evening.

Daci moved in on Payten. She turned her to her bedroom, simply stating that Payten was staying with her. Daci's house had been completed and turned back over to her.

"You're staying with me, at least for tonight, Payten. Pack what you need." Daci's hand was gentle on Payten's back as she shoved her forward. She watched as Payten seemed to move in slow motion.

Don had been watching and drew his sister away, a frown on his face.

"She's staying with you." It was a statement, not a question.

"She is. She needs this, Don. Payten's a victim of more than one crime. She has never healed from that assault. I pray that she will."

Don nodded, knowing his sister's tender heart.

—

"Paul will help. I can see her responding to him without realizing that she was. Now, he really wants to be here but he's not back until late tomorrow. Joshua is rounding up a crew to come in tomorrow and paint and clean."

"Thank you, Don." Daci turned to Joshua who stood nearby and hugged him. "What time are you thinking?"

"Around 10. Find out if Payten wants to change the colours at all." Joshua turned around as he heard a sound behind him. "Payten. I'm Joshua."

"Thank you, Joshua. This helps. As to colours, peach would be nice. I painted this green when I moved in. It needs to be refreshed. I just wasn't planning on doing it this way." Payten blinked back tears.

"It's what we do, Payten. A friend calls it being the hands and feet of Christ on earth."

Payten had been listening to him, a nod coming from her.

"He's correct. I would like to meet him some day." She looked at Joshua as he laughed. "I'm sorry?"

"It's okay. He's from another security team. They're coming in tomorrow to help. All five of them and their spouses. And before you ask, they volunteered as soon as they heard. Talk to them. They all had life and death challenges."

"They did?" Payten looked past them as she heard a tap at the door. "Toryn? You're here?"

Toryn nodded, his eyes assessing Payten.

"I am, Payten. Just wanted to make sure that you're okay. And Payten, Aidan and I will be here tomorrow as well. It's what we do for our force. You've been part of it in the past." Toryn hugged her and then stepped back beside Don, a slight nod at the other man alerting him that they needed to talk.

Payten stood by Daci's car, waiting for Daci to return. Mark approached her, trying to read her emotions and not able to.

"Daci? I had a chance to check your security feed. It went down about two hours before you arrived home."

She paled, knowing what he was saying.

"If I had left work early, I would have been here. I could have disappeared without anyone knowing!" She was horrified at that thought.

"You could have. I'm going over your house again tomorrow. A friend is bringing in steel doors for front and back. One of Richard's men does security. He'll help me go back over everything and tighten it up." His hand opened. "This was in the security system console."

Payten paled as she studied what he held. She was familiar with the object, something that was inserted into security consoles to track passwords.

"When?"

"That we can't determine. You set the system when you're not home. It could be sometime when you were home early in the week and were out in the

—

backyard. They would only need a couple of moments to do that. At any time, did you leave your front door unlocked?" He watched with sympathy as her eyes closed.

"I did. Tuesday night I was bringing out furniture from where I stored it in the garage. I didn't lock the door when I closed it, not thinking that I had to."

"From now on, you need to, Payten. They've shown that they'll take any opportunity to try and harm you."

Payten turned away, fear driving her to pace. Daci approached her, wrapping an arm around her and drawing her to the car.

"Let's head out, Payten. I think that we need a movie night. We need to forget this for a night."

"Is that even possible? I don't know that it is." Payten studied Daci, wondering why she wanted to spend time with her when she felt so dangerous.

"I do think it is. We'll watch movies, eat junk food, and then sleep. You need a night when you can forget this. Paul will be in touch, I know him that well. Talk to him. I am sure that Don has already spoken with him."

"He has. Paul sent me a text message, wishing that he could be here. He's deep into that seminar, though." Payten didn't voice her thoughts, that he shouldn't be worrying about her.

"He'll be here before you know it. Tomorrow? We'll help you get your home back to normal. You'll be overwhelmed by the teams' help. They want to do that. And with Richard's team? Two of his team are ladies."

"They are? That's unusual."

"At one time, it likely was. It's becoming more common. Richard was very careful with his ladies as he calls them. All three of the men on the team watched out for them even though they protested that they were able to take care of themselves." Daci drew to a stop in front of her garage. "Before we go in, let me pray with you, Payten."

Chapter 9

Payten was shocked at the number of people who appeared at her home the next morning. She had been warned by Daci but had not believed her. Daci was laughing at her, having known just how many people would show up.

The day passed in laughter for Payten. She felt welcomed into the two teams, not sure that she should be. Aidan wrapped an arm around his friend's shoulders, seeing the happiness on her face. He had not seen that degree of happiness ever in Payten, he thought.

"Happy, Payten?" Aidan grinned down at her.

"I am. Thank you, Aidan. You didn't have to come and help."

"But I did. You've helped out others. It's your turn." Aidan moved away, leaving Toryn moving in on her.

"Doing okay, Payten?" Toryn assessed her carefully.

"I am. Thank you, Toryn. I didn't expect this."

"I know that you didn't. It's what we do. You know that. Don and Richard? They do this for their friends. And they seem to consider you a friend. If you didn't catch it, they grew up together."

"That's what Daci said. Now, what is left to do?" Payten looked around.

—

"It's all done. Even the cleaning up is done. Now, we're heading out for a meal. Paul has just arrived. He'll be in shortly." Daci hugged her. "I am so glad to have you as a friend. Last night was fun. We need to do that again."

Payten laughed, knowing that Daci was right. She had enjoyed herself immensely.

"Thank you, Daci. It was fun." She felt an arm around her and leaned back against the man standing behind her. "And Paul is here."

"And I am. Thanks, Daci. I know that you helped arrange this."

Daci shook her head.

"Not this time. Don did that by himself. Join us for a meal. You know where we'll be." Daci walked away with a wave.

Paul hugged Payten tighter, his chin resting on the top of her head.

"Doing okay?" Paul waited for Payten to speak.

"I am. Your team and Richard's team just took over. It's good to have the house refreshed."

"It is. Now, do you want to join the others for a meal? It's your choice." Paul tilted his head to watch her face.

Payten paused, knowing that their friendship seemed to be going somewhere that she had not expected. She shrugged.

"We can, I guess. It's what you want to do."

Paul hesitated for a moment.

"It is what I would like to do. It's what you want to do that's important. If you want to stay here, send me away, and lock the door after me, that's fine. If you want to come with me to another restaurant, we can do that. Or we can join the group."

Payten turned to him, studying his face before she sighed. This seemed to be such a big decision.

"Can we just go somewhere quiet? I don't want to hurt their feelings."

Paul laughed before he hugged her once more, before reaching for her keys, watching her set her security system and then leading her from the house.

"It won't offend them at all. In fact, they likely expect us to do this." Paul tucked her into his truck and ran around to slide behind the wheel. "Do you have a preference?"

"Not really, but a good burger would be nice. I haven't had one in a while." Payten smiled as Paul laughed.

"We can do that. I know a nice little restaurant that is not too well known. I found it years ago. I lived on the streets for a while. The owner of this restaurant took me into his home and family and helped me go to college. They will welcome you."

"I didn't know that you had lived on the streets." Payten watched him closely, seeing a bit of sadness on his face.

"I did. I was in a foster home that really wasn't that great. A friend from there and I took off. I headed

---

out one day for food and was mugged, and that's when Ben found me. I lost track of my friend after that. She must think that I abandoned her."

"Her?" Payten waited for Paul to continue.

"Yes. A friend named Aideen. I wish I knew that she had survived and was safe. We just ended up parting ways without really knowing that we would. I pray that she is safe."

"Have you searched for her?"

Paul nodded, knowing that he had done what he could.

"I have. I have had to leave her with God. That's okay. He's watching out for her." Paul reached for Payten's hand as he helped her down from the truck, not letting go of it as they walked into the small restaurant.

Ben looked up from the kitchen as he heard Paul's voice, dropping the towel that he had been drying his hands on, walking towards Paul, and hugging him.

"Paul? You're okay after the other day? You did call and let us know that you were. We just needed to see you."

"I'm okay, Ben. It's not something that I would ever want to repeat though." He reached again for Payten's hand. "This is Payten. She was with me that day."

Ben just reached and hugged Payten.

"You're family, Payten. Yes, you are. Now, what would you two like to have?"

"One of your burger specials, Ben. Payten has had a craving for a burger." Paul grinned at her as he headed down the hall towards an office.

Payten looked shocked for a moment. She shook her head at Paul.

"Should we be back here? We're customers."

"It's fine, Payten. It's where I usually eat. I think that Rachel is likely to be around at some point. That's Ben's wife."

Payten simply sat as Paul gently shoved her down, her thoughts muddled for a moment, totally unlike her.

—

53

Payten walked her home a week later. It had been a busy week. Saturday had come with a word of thanks to her Heavenly Father. Paul had been away for the week, not being able to call her as he had been on a daily basis. She had received a few short texts from him. Payten sighed, wanting to see him but doubting that she would.

Hearing a tap at the door, Payten frowned. She was not expecting anyone. She cautiously crept to the door, peeking out. Of course, it would that man, but it was okay in her book. Payten unlocked her door and pulled it open. Paul simply wrapped her into a hug, the yellow roses that he held dropping down to the floor.

"Doing okay, sweetheart?" Paul loosened his hug, leaning back to look into her face. He grinned at the happy glow on it.

"I am. I didn't think that you would be back so soon. Come in."

Paul followed her, grabbing the flowers from the floor and handing them to her. He smiled as she stared at them before the happiness on her face increased.

"Thank you, Paul." She headed for the kitchen, Paul following her. "This is so sweet."

"Thank you, Payten, for being who you are. Now, are you up for a meal out?"

Payten paused before she nodded.

"That would be nice. At Ben's?"

—

"If you wish to. If not, we can find another one."

"No, Ben's is fine. He's your family."

Paul paused at her words before he nodded. Payten was correct. Ben and Rachel were his family.

"Any problems this week?" Paul waited for Payten to tie her running shoes.

"No, none. I was expecting some. Could it be because you were away?"

Paul hesitated to respond, in his mind not quite sure how to.

"It's possible, Payten. I don't know what that would be. It's possible, I guess, but I doubt it. You may have been followed."

"I likely have been. Aidan is having officers check my car when I get to work. It's locked away during the day behind fences. They sweep it again before I leave. It's getting old, very fast."

He laughed at her words, tucking her into his truck before running around it. Pulling away from the curb, he watched as a truck followed him. Memorizing the plate number, he knew that he would call it in when he could.

"Do Ben and Rachel have children of their own?" Payten was curious, knowing that Paul would hesitate to answer her.

"No, they don't. They wanted them but couldn't have any. That made it important for them when I came into their lives. I was sixteen or seventeen at the time."

"You've had a rough life, Paul, but have come through with a strong true faith."

"I have, Payten. It's what has gotten me through so much." He spun his wheel to the right suddenly, up and over a curb and then sped through an almost empty parking lot. He shot out onto the street and sped down it, turning on to other roads as he attempted to elude the vehicle behind him.

Payten gave a small scream, reaching out to grab at the arm rest. Her eyes were huge as she stared at Paul.

"What happened?" Her voice was shaky with her fear.

"We've had a tail since we left your home. They just tried to ram me. They've been watching you that closely, Payten."

"If they have been, why wait until you were here? They could have done this at any time."

Pulling to the side of a street, Paul nodded, his eyes searching for the vehicle that had been behind him. He drew in a deep breath before reaching for his phone. He placed his call before he reached for Payten's hand and began to pray. Paul knew that help was on the way. It just disturbed him that once more Payten was at risk.

Payten watched him when he had finished, a somewhat amused look on her face.

"Is this how you do your work? Run from vehicles like this?"

Paul stared at her for a moment before he began to laugh. Payten had struck again with her understated sense of humour.

"Sometimes. We try to avoid chases like this. Don doesn't like them." Paul grinned in response.

"Then, he wouldn't be too happy right now."

"He wouldn't be. I did what I needed to do. I got you away from danger." Paul watched as blue and red emergency lights appeared behind him and an officer approached him. "Ted? You're here."

Ted grinned at them for a moment before he sobered.

"I picked up the call. You were chased?"

"We were. This is the license plate number for the vehicle that tailed us from Payten's home." The two men shared a look.

"Outside her home?" Ted looked across at Payten, seeing her nodding. "Payten?"

"I've seen it around town. I just didn't know that it was around my home. Where am I to be safe?" Payten was growing angry and then sighed. *Lord, take my anger. I know that it's human to feel anger. I'm trying to trust in You, but it's hard. I worry about Paul, that he'll be hurt because of me. I don't know that I could live with myself if he is hurt.*

Chapter 11

Paul headed for Don's instead of heading for Ben's. He knew that he needed to bring in help. This had been dangerous for Payten. Paul had been afraid that he would not be able to elude the pursuers. They needed to make plans.

Payten drew in a deep breath. She was deeply afraid at this point. She didn't want to put Paul in danger but she had no idea where to go from there. Payten sighed as Paul parked in front of Don's house.

Don turned as he heard a tap at the door and then Paul's voice as he called hello.

"In the office, Paul. Didn't you just go home?"

"I did. Payten's with me. We need to talk." Paul stalked through the house, shoving Payten into a chair, and then dropping into one himself. His eyes didn't leave Payten who stared back at him.

Don's eyes bounced between the two, wondering who would win the staring contest. When it seemed that neither would give up, he smiled before he spoke.

"What happened, Paul?" Don sat back in his chair, his arms folding over his chest.

"There was a truck parked outside of Payten. It followed up. I was able to get away and did speak with Ted. However, that does not explain why or who."

"No, it doesn't. Payten, have you seen this truck?" Don waited patiently for Payten to speak, sharing a look with Paul.

—

Payten didn't stop staring at Paul. She was still trying to determine just how he had escaped the truck.

"It's been around town. I have not seen it in front of my house. That only happened when Paul appeared. So, is it after me or after Paul?"

"That's what we'll find out." Don took the slip of paper that Paul handed him. "We'll search it out, Payten. In the meantime, it seems that whoever it is has teamed the two of you up. We need to find out why."

"And there is not enough information to do that. We'll have to start digging into our background. And that means digging into our clients, too." Paul was thinking through what they needed to do.

"We know that, Paul, and we will." Don looked at Payten, finding her watching him, her eyes steady on him. "Payten, what are your thoughts?"

"My thoughts? I would work it as Aidan would. It's going to be an investigation that needs to be done. I have started making notes, thinking that this would be needed to be done."

"Good. We can get that later. For now, we need to eat. I have meat in the fridge that I want to grill. I also have fixings for a salad. How does that sound?"

"It sounds good." Payten was on her feet, heading for his kitchen, knowing that he would just tell her to go ahead.

On his feet, Paul watched Payten walk away. He turned to Don, finding Don on his feet and watching Paul in return.

"Don, what didn't you say?"

"That for some reason, both of you are in danger. We just don't know why or from whom. I reached out to Emma at Trackers. She's agreed to do some research when she can."

"She's in something urgent, then. That's fine. For now, it just seems to be threats."

"You think that the bomb was a threat?" Don had not thought of that angle but he was sure that Paul had thought it through.

"I do. It's strange that it didn't explode until we were outside. I think it had a remote trigger and that someone saw me open the door and us running. The bomb squad leader talked to me. They weren't able to retrieve very much of it but that was his guess."

"That sounds about right. We've talked about that, Paul, among ourselves. I reached out to Abe's team as well. They think along the same lines as you do."

"It's a puzzle, isn't it, Don? For now, let's put it aside. If we don't go rescue our dinner, we might not get it." Paul walked away, leaving Don shaking his head before he followed him to find that Payten had started the grill and had the meat already on it. A large salad also stood ready.

Paul drove Payten home that night, watching as the stars appeared. He didn't want to leave her on her own but he had no choice. Walking her to her door, he reached to hug her.

—

"I don't like leaving you on your own." Paul waited as she unlocked the door before he walked through the house, returning to stand in front of her.

"You need to, Paul. You need to go home. I'll be okay. The doors will be locked and the security system set."

"Okay. I'll see you in the morning." Paul dropped a kiss on her cheek and walked away, listening as Payten locked up behind him.

Payten stood for a moment, leaning against the door. A hand rested on her cheek. *Did he really just do that, Lord? Is there something going on there that I don't know about? Thank you for bringing Paul and his friends into my life. Protect them, please, dear Lord.*

Payten reached for her Bible as she curled up in the living room. She read through the verses about God's protection and His defense of her. She then turned to find verses on peace. She needed to find that. Only tonight that was not happening.

Her Bible set to one side, Payten scooted down until she was laying on the couch, a blanket pulled over herself. She slept that night, for once a sleep that was dreamless. Her hand rested against the cheek where Paul had kissed her. She needed that contact with him even in her sleep.

Paul stood at his office window, one hand resting on the window frame. He was lost in thought, trying to make sense of what had happened in the last couple of weeks. He was unable to do so, not having enough information. His own heart turned to pray for his lady,

Payten becoming very dear to him. He knew that he would spend tomorrow with her, if she would allow him to. It didn't matter what they did. It was the time together that he desired.

Chapter 12

The following Monday, Paul dropped his paperwork on the table in the board room before he headed for the kitchen and poured himself a mug of coffee. He turned as he heard footsteps approaching. Thomas and Caleb had appeared, reaching for their own coffee before turning to Paul.

"Paul. You're healing?" Thomas was concerned about his friend.

"I am. It's just frustrating not knowing who it is that is after us. Payten doesn't have any idea either." Paul headed for the board room and pulled back his chair. He greeted Mark and Joshua, knowing that Don was around somewhere in the building.

Don stood just out of sight in the hallway, hearing his team joking around and teasing one another. He could hear also the underlying emotions in Paul's voice. He stepped into the room, heading for his chair, his men calling out greetings to him.

Spending time in prayer was how the day would start for the team. They needed that contact with one another.

Don raised his head, studying each man ending with his eyes on Paul. They didn't have enough information to determine what was going on and that was a fact.

"Paul? Where do things stand with you and with Payten?"

"Not where we would like it. We tried to spend some time on it yesterday but didn't make much of a headway into it." Paul rubbed at the side of his head.

"What can you tell us?" Thomas turned to him. "And what can we work on?"

"For now? We're trying to figure out if we've had contact with one another at some point. We haven't found that. We'll be looking at our families and working out from there."

Mark reached for the paperwork that Paul held up. Looking through it, he nodded. Paul had made a good start for them. Mark was on his feet, heading for the copier to make copies for each of them.

"We'll work on it, Paul, as we can. How be we do that and try and meet on Friday afternoon?" Mark looked over at Don who was nodding. "Would Payten be available?"

"No, I think that she has to work that day. I'll ask her." Paul's phone was out as he sent off a text message, setting his phone carefully on the table. "It has us puzzled, guys. How do we find out what is happening and why?"

"That's a good question, Paul." Don leaned forward, his forearms resting on the table. "I spoke with Richard last night about something else. He was asking about you. He's worried."

"What did he have to say?" Paul kept his eyes on Don, hoping that he had some answers for him.

"Richard? He would like to meet with us, if we can figure out a time to do that. You know what he and his team went through. He's hoping that he can help."

"I am sure that he can." Paul blew out a breath, his phone vibrating catching his attention. He frowned as he read Payten's message. "Payten's free on Friday. She's asked for a leave of absence for the next three weeks. She doesn't feel safe at work. Does that make sense?"

"It does. If someone is after her, they could certainly get to someone that she works with. It's been done before." Mark tilted his head to study Paul.

"It has been. And Payten did wonder if someone who worked with her was behind this." Paul was torn, wanting to be with Payten but knowing that he needed to work. *Lord, help me out here, please. I want to be with my lady but I have to be with my team. I just don't know how to do this.*

Caleb and Joshua shared a look before Caleb nodded. They had a good idea of what Paul was thinking.

"Paul. What are your plans?"

"I have no idea, Caleb. This is all new territory for us. I was hoping that we could pool our thoughts and figure it out." Pau rubbed at his head, a headache building behind his eyes.

"We can try, but for now, we need to look at the assignment upcoming for us." Don handed around the documents that he prepared for the team.

Discussion was deep as the men read through the material. Caleb frowned for a moment before he was on his feet, heading for his office and then back in his seat. He opened the folder that he had retrieved, reading through what he had retrieved in his research.

"Don, there is a problem, I think, with this assignment. Here." Caleb handed over his research.

Don frowned for a moment, his eyes on Caleb.

"What can you give me briefly?"

"This man? He is not who he says he is. I just found it out this morning. I had forgotten for a moment that he was our assignment for next week."

Don nodded, knowing that Caleb would be contrite for that but that he had provided the information that Don required to make a decision about whether they continued with the assignment. Reading over the investigation that Caleb had done, Don paused, his eyes on the men as they too read through it. He nodded once more, rising to his feet and moving to his office. A phone call to the police officer who had arranged the assignment took only a few moments. The assignment was canceled. Don sat for a few moments, his head bowed in prayer. Something was going on with his team, something threatening them all. He just didn't have a handle on it.

On his feet once more, he returned to the board room, standing for a moment in the hallway to listen to the team. He could hear the tension in their voices, not towards one another but towards the circumstances, particularly what Paul was facing.

Paul rose, heading for the door to search for Don. His phone was in his hand. He paused for a moment to study Don before he spoke.

"Don?"

"Paul? I've canceled the assignment for next week. We're not taking any chances on it. Now, we'll work on what you and Payten are facing. You said that she's off work?"

"She is. She didn't want to endanger anyone there. There's also a suspicion that someone she works with is involved. I put in a call to Emma." Emma was a friend of theirs but also had an investigative business where she could find information on anyone that no one else could find.

"That works. We'll get together with you two on Monday, if she's available, and see what we can find. It's going to be tough keeping you two safe."

"I know. I hate this for her." Paul walked away, his emotions out of control for the moment.

Chapter 13

Monday found Payten walking towards Don's building, her hand tight in Paul's. She had not expected him to show up that morning. Paul had simply grinned at her and walked her to his truck, shutting the door behind her. He had watched her through the window, seeing how she was shifting on the seat.

Payten was not sure about being there. She knew of Don's team but had had no contact with them or not much of one. She stood for a moment in the conference room, Paul leaving for a moment to grab their coffee. Thomas watched her for a moment before he entered the room, his footsteps on the hardwood floor startling her.

Thomas grinned, knowing that he had startled her without meaning to.

"I'm sorry, Payten. I didn't mean to scare you. I'm Thomas." He set his mug and paperwork down and reached to shake her hand. "Paul's around?"

"He is. Somewhere. I feel as if I have been abandoned." Payten was grumpy. She sighed. She would need to apologize, she knew. *Lord, I could use some help here. I'm out of my comfort zone. Thank you.*

Paul reached to wrap an arm around her, feeling her leaning against him as the other men approached and greeted her. She was uncertain at that, not

—

knowing them. She turned her face up to Paul, seeing him watching her in turn. He gave a quick grin at her.

Don watched from outside the doorway, a frown on his face for a moment. He looked at the other men, finding them studying Payten as well.

Paul reached to pull back a chair for Payten, seating her. He disappeared for a moment, returning with hot drinks for them both. He sat beside her, his hand reaching to hers. Payten stared at their linked hands for a moment, knowing that Paul was saying something to her and also to his friends.

Don raised his head at last after they had spent their normal time in prayer. He as well as his team knew that they would not have been as protected in their works without bathing themselves in prayer. He turned once more to Paul, finding him ready to defend his lady against them if that was necessary. Don's head ducked for a moment as he hid a grin.

"Paul? What news have you discovered?" Mark broke the silence, causing Payten to jump and stare at him.

"What have I discovered? Not a lot. This situation is puzzling. Payten and I have discussed it over and over. Payten?" Paul's voice caught at Payten's attention.

"Paul? You had a question?" Payten turned to him, not sure what to say.

"We do. We asked what you have discovered and what you can share with us." Caleb grinned at her. "That is, if you want to."

—

"I really haven't discovered anything. I have no idea who in my past would be after me." Payten drew in a shuddering breath. "This is hard. I see this kind of stuff that involves others in my work. Going through this? I'm not sure that I can continue with my work. And that sucks, big time."

"You may need to take a break from it." Joshua spoke up, a concerned look on his face. "How be you tell us about yourself? We would like to count you as a friend."

"You would? You're not just saying that?" As the men shook their heads, Payten sighed with relief. "I thought that you would blame me for what happened with Paul."

"It's not your fault, Payten." Mark nodded at Paul. "Paul's involved in what is going on. So, if it involves Paul, it involves all of us. We protect and defend any ladies in our lives. That goes without saying. We don't want to see you hurt, not any more than you have been. We'll work on this as we can. We call in friends who will help. If we need to stick you away somewhere to keep you safe, we'll do that. We don't want any of this for you. Ever."

Payten had sat up straighter as Mark had spoken. Paul had told her that but she had not wanted to believe him. Now, she did. A tear trickled down her cheek, Paul's finger wiping it away.

"I'm sorry. I didn't realize that. What can I do to help?" Payten sniffed, trying to control herself, taking with thanks the large white handkerchief that Thomas handed her.

"We need a list of who you work with, your friends outside of work, your professors from college. Places that you have lived. Your parents' names and vital information. Your other family members. Anything that you can think of that might have a bearing on it." Mark shoved a pad of paper and a pen towards her.

Payten nodded at last, sniffing as she tried to control her emotions. Her hand reached for the pen, a frown on her face. Paul was on his feet, walking from the room, his emotions overcoming him for a moment.

Caleb followed him, a hand resting on his shoulder for a moment before he prayed for his friend.

"Paul, what more can we do?"

"I don't know, Caleb. I really don't. I have my own list for us to work through. It's on the table where I was sitting."

Caleb turned slightly as he heard a sound, seeing Thomas there before Thomas nodded and headed to sit where Paul had been. Thomas reached for Paul's paperwork, reading through Paul's writing before he was on his feet to copy it for them all. He handed it around, his eyes pausing on Payten for a moment. They were all worried about Paul and Payten, without knowing exactly why. All that they can do at the present time was work through what they had and try and protect Paul and Payten as much as they could.

Paul returned to his seat, a hand reaching out for Payten's, finding her reaching for his hand. The other five in the room with them exchanged glances, nodding. Paul had found his lady, they decided, and they would do all they could to defend her for him.

Chapter 14

By the end of that week, Paul was frustrated. They had not found any information of anyone who was after himself or after Payten. She had returned to work, mid-week, the sudden illness of a co-worker necessitating that. He didn't like it. Payten had just stared at him when he commented on that and walked away. Paul had stood for a moment and then ran after. His hand on her arm stopped her forward march. She was angry and frustrated. Those emotions were ones that he was fighting daily to give to God.

He paced on the sidewalk in front of Payten's house that Friday afternoon. It was past time when she should have been home. He pulled out his phone to check his messages. Payten had not sent a text since the one that he had received two hours before, just to let him know that she was leaving and would be taking her usual route home. Paul ran for his truck, heading for the police department, following that route. There was no sign of her or her car.

Parking outside of the department, Paul ran for the door and slid to a stop at the front desk. The officer there frowned at him.

"Paul?" The question in the officer's voice shook Paul for a moment.

"Payten? Has she left? She said that she was leaving two hours ago. She hasn't arrived home yet." Paul was growing increasingly worried.

"Payten? She has already."

—

"That's what I thought." Paul was gone again before the officer could stop him. His phone was out. "Don? Payten's disappeared on her way home. It's been two hours since she said that she was leaving. I'm heading back towards her home."

"Paul! Wait! What route?" Don was on the move, heading for his own truck, ready to go on a search.

Paul gave the route before he headed back towards Payten's, eyes in constant motion. He drew in a deep breath as he arrived back at her home. She was not there. Paul was out of his truck, walking the property, not seeing her. Hearing the sounds of a vehicle door closing, Paul ran for the front of the house, praying that it was her. Instead it was Aidan and Toryn.

"Paul? Any sign of her?" Toryn had been praying that she was home.

"Not a one. Don and the guys are out there searching. I didn't see any sign on the route that she told me that she would take. She's been doing that, letting me know which route she's traveling back and forth. I hadn't been able to get here until it had been almost ninety minutes. I thought maybe she had stopped at a store and was delayed."

"I have officers searching as well, Paul." Toryn moved towards her house, a key in his hand. "Payten asked me to take a key last week and had me set my own security code. Let me go through her home." Toryn disappeared inside, leaving Aidan and Paul to stare at one another.

Don walked towards Paul, Thomas at his side. A group text had had the team scrambling to search. The results had not been what Don had hoped for.

"Paul? Any word yet?" Don stopped beside Aidan. "And who's in the house?"

"Toryn is. Payten gave him a key last week. And no, no word. Not yet." Paul was worried and frustrated. "Have the guys found anything yet?"

"No, not yet." Don turned away to take a call, finding a friend with his own security team on the line.

"Don? How are you?"

"I'm fine, Richard, but I don't understand why you are calling."

"Abe reached out to me. He's been trying to reach Paul and hasn't been able to. In fact, he hasn't been able to reach any of your team."

"That is bizarre." Don searched his missed calls. "He called when we were in a meeting. We hadn't been out too long when Paul called."

"That's why then. He's really worried about Paul. He said that Emma has information for him on Payten and himself. He said that he's heading your way tomorrow and could I find out if you and your team would be around."

"We will be." Don paused for a moment, biting at his lip. "Richard, what is your team up to tomorrow?"

"We're all heading your ways, spouses included. I was going to call you this evening to see if that works. We'll help search if we need to."

"Thanks, Richard. Meet at my house."

Paul walked towards Richard, Thomas at his side. Worry was on Paul's face. Don knew that it was not usual for his emotions to be that raw and open.

"Any sign of her in the house?" Don waited patiently for Paul to speak.

"Not since this morning. Toryn said that there were some dishes in the sink but other than that? Nothing seems out of the ordinary. She's just not here."

"I see. None of the other guys have found her." Don paused for a moment, his eyes on the distance. "Would she have stopped somewhere?"

Paul shrugged, not sure of that. She might have, he thought. He just wasn't sure if she would have

Toryn approached the men, Aidan heading for his vehicle. There had been word come to the front desk of a car similar to Payten's found in the downtown area, heavily damaged. Aidan was heading that way to confirm if it was hers and if she was around there anywhere. He was reluctant to say anything, not wanting to raise the men's hopes. Don caught his eye before Don nodded.

Paul walked away, not letting Toryn speak with him. He didn't want to hear that Payten was dead and was not coming back to him. He didn't think that he could handle that. Mark walked beside him, not willing to let him be on his own. Mark saw Daci approaching them, Paul hesitating as he saw her.

"Daci? You're here?" Paul knew that Don would have reached out to her.

"I am, Paul. You need my support as does Payten when we find her."

"And you're sure about that?" Paul wanted his lady there, wanted to defend her, and just wasn't able to.

Chapter 15

On her way home that afternoon, Payten had been happy. Paul had promised to meet her at her home. They had agreed to go out for a meal, Payten still not sure how safe that they were. She was not oblivious to her surroundings. Instead, she was focused on her evening and then planning her weekend. That Paul would be a part of it was a given, she thought.

A jolt from a vehicle striking the back of her car caused her to scream. Payten stared at the rearview mirror before she was speeding away. She would not stop but instead, would try and find her way back to her work. Only that way was blocked from her by construction. Heading for the downtown area, she felt her car struck numerous times.

Panicked, Payten floored the gas pedal and took off, heading for a building where she knew that she would be safe. She flung open the door to her parked car, grabbing at her purse, and fleeing from there. She ran, panic adding flight to her feet, searching for an area to hide. Another scream came from her as a body appeared in her line of sight.

Payten tried to avoid the hand that reached for her. Unable to do so, she fought the man as he pulled her from the street and into a building. He shoved her into a room, pulling the door closed behind her, and then just crouched in the doorway. He could hear Payten pounding at the door, calling for him to let her out.

—

Realizing that she would not be able to escape through the door, Payten spun, her eyes searching the dimness of the room. She paced it, looking for any way out and finding none. What she found was a hidden crevice, just wide enough for her to step inside and out of view of the room. She spun, her eyes on the door before she looked up. *This was You, God. You sent that man to help me and had me placed here. I can hide, can't I?*

A disturbance and shouting outside the door had Payten spinning that way and then running to duck into the crevice. Her hand covered her mouth to stop her screams. She heard the door fly open to slam against the wall, shaking the room with the force of it. The loud shouts and curses sent her into even more of a cowering heap. She recognized one of the voices. A co-worker that she had trusted had betrayed her.

The man slowly raised himself from the floor. The attack had taken him by surprise. The three men had appeared in front of him, surrounding him. Their demands as to where Payten was had been met with his silence. The blow from behind him had sent him to the dirty, debris-strewn floor to lie still while the men searched for Payten. He was on his feet, heading into the room. Not seeing Payten, he was worried until he heard the slight sound of a whimper. His eyes closed. Payten was safe.

Payten jumped as she felt a hand on her arm, drawing her back out into the room. Her eyes were huge as she stared at the man.

"Justin? That was you?"

"It was, Payten. They knocked me down and out. Are you okay?" Justin was worried about Payten.

"I am, I think. Who were they?" Payten paced, not able to stand still.

"I don't know. I saw them following you when you left your car. I couldn't let them get to you. Now, we need to get you home." Justin stopped in the shadows, watching the activity around her car. "Someone reported this."

"They did. I need to get home, Justin. Except my car is destroyed. Did they do that?" Payten stared at it in shock.

"I would think so." Justin's eyes narrowed as he studied the officers. "Aidan's here."

"He is? He'll get me home." Payten made a move to go around Justin. Only his hand kept her in place. "Justin?"

"They'll be here, Payten, watching your vehicle. If you go towards Aidan, you won't make it. Come on. This way. I'll get you home. Or do you want to go to Paul's?" He grinned at her look of disbelief.

"How did you know about that?" Payten kept pace with Justin's rapid steps.

"Word's out on the streets, Payten. Everyone is looking out for you and Paul. They're trying to find out who is behind this but haven't as yet." He pointed to a beaten-up old car. "In there."

Payten slipped into the car, crouching down as Justin asked her to. He pulled away, eyes moving to try

—

and spot anyone. A hand lifted as an older man shook his head.

"We're safe for now, Payten. You can sit up." Justin drove away, intent on reaching Payten's house. He pulled to a stop near her home, his eyes on the activity surrounding it. "Someone reported you missing, Payten."

Payten nodded, a troubled look on her face.

"More than likely Paul. We were to meet here when he finished work."

Justin was around the car, opening the door, and pulling Payten out. He walked her towards her home, stopping to let her move away from him. He backed up to lean against his car, seeing the instant that Paul spotted Payten.

Paul's instincts told him that someone new was approaching him. He spun, his eyes on Payten before he yelled, startling everyone with him, leaving the officers reaching for their weapons. He raced towards Payten, simply sweeping her into a hug. Her tears wet his shirt.

"You're okay? You're not hurt?" Paul refused to let go of her

"I'm fine, Paul. Except I can't breathe." Payten's tear-stained face turned up to him as he loosened his grip. "I'm okay. I will need to talk to someone, but for now? Can we go inside?"

"We can and we will."

Surrounded by officers and with Paul's arm around her, Payten was led to her home, taken inside, and then the door closed and locked. She stared around at Paul's team as they gathered close to her, Don standing with his arm around his sister.

"Praise God that you're home. Payten? What happened?" Toryn stood there as well, ready to speak with her.

"Someone tried to kidnap me. I managed to get away and hit the downtown area. Someone hid me until it was safe to leave. He brought me home." Tears once more clouded her eyes before she felt Paul's arms around her and his whispered prayer.

Chapter 16

Daci stepped back from Payten's bedroom, knowing that Payten was cleaning up and changing into other clothes. She prayed for her friend, not sure what had happened. She turned to find Paul standing about five feet from her, his gaze flickering between Daci and the closed bedroom door.

"Daci?" His question was hesitant, not his usual strong confident tone.

"She's getting cleaned up, Paul. Come. I know that Don and the team are working on a meal for us. She'll need that whether she feels as if she can eat or not. She also needs to talk to Aidan. He's back around?"

"He is. You're right. He will need that." Paul's hands ran through his hair. "I have no idea where this is going, Daci. I just fear for Payten and her life. And I still can't see how we connected other than through church."

"We get that, Paul. We all do." Aidan spoke from behind him, causing Paul to hesitate before he turned to face the detective. "Now, how be we head for the kitchen? There's a meal waiting for you. I'll speak with Payten and then send her out to eat." Aidan walked past them, heading for Payten who now stood in the hallway, her hair wrapped in a towel from her shower. "Payten? Where can we meet?"

Payten pointed to her office, heading that way, stopping for a moment as Paul wrapped her in a hug

—

and prayed for her. He sent her on her way, a kiss to her temple. Payten's hand itched to rest at that spot, but that would wait until she was on her own. She had not been expecting that. *Did we just go somewhere with our relationship, Lord? I value his friendship. It seems as if we're heading to being more than friends, but I don't know that for sure. Please protect my friend, dear Lord. I don't want to see him hurt or see his family and friends hur*t.

Aidan sat across from Payten, his laptop out as he prepared to take her statement. He had studied her car, seeing the damage that had been done to it. He was glad that she had not been in it. She would have disappeared for good, he was certain. The damage done to the car expressed the men's anger at her disappearance.

"Aidan? Where do I start?" Payten rubbed her hands along her jean legs, uncertainty in her motions.

"From when you left work. What happened, Payten? This is not you to disappear." Aidan continued to wait patiently for Payten to speak.

"I don't know, Aidan. I finished what I had to for today. I was done about thirty minutes early and just used that time to clean up and tidy up my area. We have to do that on a daily basis. When I was done, I clocked out and headed for my car. Jack searched my car and then let me out. I was driving home on one of my usual routes. I could see that I was being followed. They hit me from behind. The construction on Oak wouldn't let me take that route. I sped away, heading for the downtown area. I parked and ran. Justin found me and hid me. I don't want to say where, as it may

---

compromise his safety. I could hear angry voices talking to him and then the men searching. When they were gone, he took me towards my car. I was told that you were there but couldn't go towards you. Justin wouldn't let me. He brought me to my home instead." Payten blinked as she remembered the fear that had grown in her as she was running from her car. It had been overwhelming. Payten could not pray, knowing instead that the Holy Spirit was praying for her.

"It's okay, Payten. You did the right thing. Your car was destroyed in anger, we think, because they could not find you. It's a warning. Now, about your work? Do you know of any of your co-workers who might have a grudge against you or want you to leave?" Again, Aidan waited patiently for Payten to think through what he had asked her. He knew her well enough to know that she needed that time.

Shaking her head, Payten sighed before she spoke. This was difficult to do.

"Not offhand, Aidan. There was one worker who left about six months ago. He never really fit into the group or the work. We all wondered why he chose that line of work." She looked up at him, a frown on her face. "Is it him?"

"We don't know, Payten. I know who you mean. We've been looking at everyone in the lab and their families. You have been honest with me, providing me with as many names as you can. I know that it is difficult for you. You're an orphan. Did you spend any time on the streets?" A thought crossed Aidan's mind that perhaps this was the link that they were searching for.

Payten shook her head, her frown deepening.

"No, I didn't. I was in a number of foster homes. I seemed be moved every six to eight months. I couldn't understand it. The last one? It was brutal. They only had foster children to work for them. Once you were eighteen and they received no money for you, you were on your own. I moved out as soon as I was eighteen. I had been working part-time. Lucy from the church took me in until I graduated from college and could move out on my own. I miss her. She was a wonderful lady." Payten paused for a moment. "Her death? She wasn't ill, had no diseases. Was her death natural?"

Aidan nodded again. Payten had taken up a thought that he was investigating.

"We're looking into that, Payten. We had the same thought. And that last foster family? They were charged when one of their foster children died under suspicious circumstances in the last year. We're reaching out to everyone who was there. You're on the list to talk to." His hand raised as her mouth opened to speak, causing her to snap it closed once more. "We'll talk, Payten. I'm not the one investigating that. Lila is. She's aware of what's happening with you. She said that she'll reach out to you next week."

"Thank you, Aidan. I thought that no one cared about that. I had no one to defend me against their demands and abuse. It's the same with that incident at college. I didn't think that I had a defender until that man stepped in. Do you know who he is?"

Aidan nodded. He knew who it was and had spoken to that man. Unknown to either Paul or Payten, Samuel was married to a friend of Paul's, Aideen. He would bring the two of them together in the next few days. Both couples needed to know of their connection to one another.

"That's it for now, Payten. Paul is waiting for you in the kitchen or the hallway. He will not have eaten until you do. Go and find him." Aidan stood, watching Payten as she hesitated for a moment. "He's interested, Payten. He's going slow, knowing that you need the time. But I can see the two of you together. You're two parts of a whole." Aidan prayed for his friends, knowing that God would defend them both but would not prevent them from going through a rough time if it was in His will for them.

Payten shot him a startled look before she almost ran from the office, finding Paul waiting down the hallway just as Aidan had predicted. She was swept into his arms, close to his heart, and found that she felt safe and cherished and loved, something that she had not felt in many years.

Chapter 17

Paul's eyes were steady on Payten as she spoke with his team mates as they ate. She had moved her chair as close to him as she could. He had smiled to himself at that. *Yes,* he thought, *she is my lady. She's letting me know that. I don't want to hurt her or see her hurt. I just don't know to protect her against what we don't know. Please protect my lady, Lord. I don't know if I can handle it if she's hurt any more than she has been.*

Payten knew that the men were curious as to what had happened to her. Toryn and Aidan had left but not before praying with her. She appreciated that. Paul's hand covered hers, keeping her in her chair as Thomas and Daci cleared the table. Don's eyes were on her as well before they shifted to watch Paul.

"Payten, what can you tell us?" Caleb spoke, his hand reaching for his notepad and pen.

"Not a lot. I didn't see the men. They tried to force me off the street but I managed to get away. Justin found me in the downtown area and then hid me. There were three of them. I could hear their voices. They were rough and sounded as if they were smokers. I think that Justin was hurt by them. I just don't have that confirmation."

"Your car?" Joshua picked up on that.

"They destroyed it. Aidan said that it's a write-off. It's been taken to the police garage. I'll need to call my insurance agent." Payten wiped at her face, unable to contain her tears. "I don't get why. Who is doing this?"

"We'll find them, Payten. That's a guarantee to you. We have friends who are working on it as well. I don't know if you would know Emma and Abe and his team or Richard and his team. They are all concerned about this. They know Paul. Through Paul, they know you."

"Thank you. I didn't know that there were others helping us." Payten leaned against Paul who had wrapped an arm around her.

"Paul? I need to run a name by you." Don spoke up, knowing that when he named the person, Paul would want to head to Elmton. "When we were discussing names yesterday, you mentioned a lady by the name of Aideen who had been in the last foster home with you. You two walked away from it and you lost touch with her."

"I did. She was a good friend, Don. I often wondered what happened to her. I have prayed that she survived and is married to someone who could see past the foster child and love her for who she is." Paul's eyes narrowed as he caught the look on Don's face. "Don? Do you know where she is?"

"I do. She is in Elmton. Aideen had an adventure just as it appears that you and Payten are off on. She is married to a friend of Richard's. Samuel."

Paul drew in a deep breath. He was glad to hear that Aideen was safe.

"She's been that close? I tried to find her but couldn't. I just wanted to make sure that she was safe."

"And she is. In fact. Richard asked me if you were the Paul that she had been in foster care with. One of the ladies on his team asked him."

"We'll need to get together." Paul frowned harder at Don. "What did you do?"

"Richard and his team and their spouses are heading for my place tomorrow. Samuel and Aideen are coming as well. Samuel is a title searcher and may aid us in what we are looking at. You know that we have a number of addresses to research. When he heard it was for you, he gladly volunteered."

"Wow! I didn't expect that!" Paul's arm tightened around Payten as he felt her shifting to look at him. "Aideen is a special lady, Payten, but she is just a friend." His eyes spoke to her from his heart, showing her his feelings for her. She drew in a breath, not quite sure that she was reading him correctly. "You'll get to meet the lady who was in danger without us knowing that. I know that for a fact. We took to the streets when it became unbearable to remain in the foster system. I headed out to find food one day, was injured, and taken in by Ben. I could not track her after that. She hid herself well."

"She did. She had to. Richard was involved in protecting her and Samuel. He hasn't said much but he did say it was brutal what she had been put through." Don paused, his eyes on Payten. "We need to head out, Payten. Let's pray with you before we do."

—

Paul turned away from the front door, hunting for Payten. She was standing in the kitchen, staring at the calendar on the wall. He didn't think that she was even aware of what she was looking at. His arms around her had her relaxing back against him.

"Payten? What do we do with you?" Paul was not expecting an answer from her.

Payten shrugged, not sure what to say.

"I don't know, Paul. I really don't know. What can we do to solve this now?"

"We are working on it, sweetheart. I don't know what we can do. We need to find that one link or one person that we can use to solve it. And that means a lot of research and investigation."

"I wish it was all over, Paul. You can't move on with your life until it is." Payten felt his arms tighten around her. "Paul?"

Paul bit at his bottom lip. This was not how he had planned on talking with her about his feeling. He only knew that he had to.

"Payten? You are a very beautiful and loving lady who I am privileged to call my friend. I sense that you are welcoming my friendship. I want to date you, to see where this goes. I don't date. I didn't want to, not wanting the ladies to think that there might be something there that isn't. Would you be willing to be my lady?" He waited for her to digest his word, hardly daring to breathe.

Payten grew still, wonder in her heart at his words. She had dreamed of this, of having a man interested in dating her. There had been interest on some men's part but she had not felt led by God to date them. Now, here was Paul, asking that of her.

Payten nodded, unable to speak for a moment. She felt his arms tighten just a bit. In that motion, she felt his love and determination to defend her at all costs.

"I will, Paul. I will." She reached to wipe away a tear. "Did God bring us together?"

"I am sure that He did, sweetheart. I am sure of that." Paul prayed for guidance in their path together before he reached for her hand. He walked towards the front door. "Lock up after me. I'll be here in the morning. If you need me or any of my team, call us. We don't care what time of day or night it is." He dropped a kiss on her cheek before closing the door behind him.

Payten stood, her hand on the lock that she had twisted. She was locked in for the night in her home. But in her heart, she could feel the loosening of the lock that she had placed it under. Paul was working his way into her life and heart. She could not deny that nor did she want to.

Chapter 18

The next morning, Payten stood in her backyard, anger on her face. Someone had been in there overnight. She just had not heard them. Her backyard was destroyed. Her plants that were just starting to grow were all torn from the ground and tossed around. Any ornaments that she ha in the gardens were smashed. Her swing was destroyed, the pieces thrown around.

Payten wiped away the tears that trickled down her cheeks. Her sleep had been troubled the night before. She had not gotten a lot of sleep. Her emotions were in a turmoil. *Did I have to leave my work and my town and my new friends, Lord? I can't do this. I need this over but it just keeps snowballing.*

Paul had not received an answer to his knocks at the door. Worried about his lady, he had searched for her, coming around the house to find her just standing in the middle of the yard, her face buried in her hands. What had happened here? And when? It had been fine when they had all left the night before.

Payten jumped as she felt Paul's arms around her before he turned her into his shoulder. He just held her as she sobbed, his chin resting on her head. His eyes studied the damage done to her yard before he sighed. He turned her towards the house, an arm around her guiding her inside. Once inside, he shoved her into a chair, crouching down beside her.

"Sweetheart? What happened? You're okay?" Paul's worry was evident in his voice.

——

"I don't know any more, Paul. I think that I'm just bringing danger to everyone. I didn't hear anything last night. You would think that I would have, given the damage that was done. But then it was windy last night."

"Did you sleep at all?" Paul refused to move from her side until he knew that she was okay.

"Not really." She sighed, her eyes on his face, seeing the worry and concern on it. "I'll need to look at the security feed, won't I?"

"You will. Let me call it in. We'll need to contact your insurance agent."

Payten was on her feet, heading for the coffee pot. She needed a cup of coffee and a strong one at that.

"I know. I left a message last night on his voice mail about the car. Now this! Who did I hurt or anger, Paul? Can you tell me that?" Her words spit out in anger, not directed at Paul but at what she was facing. "I want this over. I need that. You need that. I don't know if it's me or you."

"We don't know that yet, sweetheart. We're working on that. It's just that we need that one piece of information. We're praying for that. But it is in God's timing."

"I know that it is. I just wish that He'd hurry up and give us that." Payten was confident enough in her faith to know that she was not being disrespectful. She had many conversations with God as her Abba Father, just as she would have had with her earthly father.

Paul grinned at her before he was on his feet, heading for the door to greet the patrol officer. A few quick words with the officer ensued before the officer was heading around the house.

Payten stood at her back door, watching the officers move around her yard. She recognized members of the crime scene team taking evidence. She was frustrated beyond anything that she had ever felt before. She didn't want this. In fact, Payten wanted just to pack up and run. Only, there was a man standing right behind her who she could see in the door window who would not let her.

"Paul? Why this? Why destroy my home and property?" Payten was near tears.

"I don't know, Payten. That's what we're working on. And it does take time." Paul wrapped her in his arms, his chin on the top of her head. "I know it's hard, sweetheart. I know that. I just want to take you away somewhere that you would be safe. And I can't do that. We need to work this through and bring whoever it is to justice. Somehow, I think that it's going to take some time. And I am afraid for you. I don't want to lose you or have you hurt."

"I get that, Paul. I don't want you hurt any more than you have been. And just how do we do that?" Payten moved to open the door, stepping outside as she saw Aidan. "Aidan?"

"Payten? This is not how to start your day." Aidan pointed towards the house. "Back inside. I want to view your security footage."

Payten nodded and headed for her office. She sat in front of her computer monitor and pulled up the program. She moved aside to let Aidan sit in her chair. She paced, her eyes on him, watching closely for any reaction from him.

"Aidan? When did they come through?" Payten finally had to ask.

"Around two or so. You were sleeping?" Aidan looked up at her, seeing her nod. "One of the few times that you slept, I would imagine. I'll need a copy of this, Payten. You can give it to me or I can ask for a warrant. Maybe we should do that, just to be on the up and up."

Payten nodded before she just shrugged.

"Go ahead and take it, Aidan." Payten walked away, leaving Aidan staring after her and then staring at Paul. "Paul?"

Paul shook his head.

"I'm sorry, Aidan. I don't know what to say. I can get her to come back if you need her to."

"No, that's fine. I'll just copy this and email it to myself." Aidan did that, his thoughts racing at the same time. "Paul? What are your thoughts? I know that your team has been working on this."

"We have been, Aidan, as we can. We have not had a lot of time due to being away on assignments. There is not a lot to find out right now. Friends are heading in today to help. And someone named Emma Finlay will be forwarding you a lot of material." Paul grinned at Aidan.

"She already it. Toryn says that she's a consultant with us. I just have to find the time to go through it all."

"Look at the top sheet of each file. She'll have put in a concise recap of what she has found. That's how she does it." Paul walked away, intent on finding Payten, not expecting to find her shaking in fear as she held an envelope that she had pulled from the mailbox. He gently reached for it, set it to one side, and wrapped her tight to his heart. His prayer rose to Heaven, begging God to protect and defend his lady.

Chapter 19

Paul watched later that morning as his team and Richard's team and their spouses mingled inside and outside Payten's house. The plan to meet at Don's house had shifted to Payten's given what had happened overnight. Payten was with Daci, taking stock of what she needed to replace in her gardens. He knew it was difficult for her. Richard paused beside Paul, a hand resting on his shoulder for a moment.

"Your team cleaned up her yard?" Richard was sure that they had. He just had to ask.

"They did. They were shocked, to say the least. I was. We'll need to work with her on refurbishing her yard." Paul was sad at that thought.

Richard nodded. He knew that it would take time for her yard to come back to where it had been yesterday.

"We'll do what we can to help. Now, for you, Paul? What can we do for you?" Richard watched him closely, knowing how close to the edge he was feeling.

Paul shrugged. He had no idea what he needed or even wanted for himself. His thoughts were focused on Payten. He didn't turn as a couple approached him. He was lost in thought as Payten walked into his arms.

"Paul?" A soft voice caught at his memories. "Paul? Is that you?"

Paul's eyes closed for a moment. It sounded like Aideen but how could that be possible? He felt Payten

---

turning him to face the couple. His eyes opened as he focused on the lady.

"Aideen? You're here?" Paul reached to hug her before he shook the hand of the man with Aideen. "I lost track of you."

"I know. I looked for you but could never find you. What happened?" Aideen's hand covered her mouth for a moment as she tried to control her tears.

Samuel wrapped his arm around her, worry for her on his face.

"I was hurt that day and couldn't get back to you. A couple here in town found me and took me in. I searched for you. You left town?"

"I did. But not right away. It wasn't until I was in danger that I fled. I reached out to Samuel's father and he helped me. This is my husband, Samuel Harding. Samuel, this is the Paul that I've told you about. We were in foster care together."

"Is there something that we can do to help? Richard told us what happened." Samuel was concerned about his wife's long-lost friend.

"Right now? I'm not sure what to do. We were planning on working through what we had to see what we could find. You're welcome to help." Paul just wrapped his arm tighter around Payten, needing that contact with her.

"And we will." Aideen moved past Paul to Payten. "Payten? May I call you that?" When Payten nodded, Aideen hugged her. "Come, show me your yard. I see Daci is here. You've met the other ladies.

———

Talk to us about what you want to do in the yard. This is an opportunity to put in what you want and redesign it.”

“I know. I just don’t know if I have the heart to do that.” Payten walked away with Aideen and Daci. The men watching her could see her discouragement and defeat in how she held herself.

Paul watched her walk away before he spoke. He knew that Don and Richard were nearby.

“Don? What have you found?” Paul didn’t turn. He knew that his team was there and that the men on Richard’s team were there as well as the two husbands of his lady team members.

“Not what you want to hear, Paul.” Don sighed. This is not how the day was to go, not by a long shot. “The gardens? Her swing? I am surprised that she didn’t hear them. They were very violent as they tore everything apart. God protected her in that.”

“He did.” Richard agreed. He was running scenarios in his mind, trying to determine what they could do to help. “What do you want to do, Paul, right now? Payten needs someone to defend her.”

“She does. And I can’t do it, not the way that I want to.” Paul was frustrated. His eyes were on Payten and the other ladies. “She’s in danger, guys. How do we find out who it is?”

Timothy, one of Richard’s men, spoke up, his eyes on his friends.

“It’s tough to be in this situation, Paul. We can understand to a certain extent what you and Payten are going through. Where can we work through the paperwork that you have?"

"Payten's office. She's already said that was fine." Paul turned to head that way, not seeing the compassionate looks sent his way.

The men followed him, except for Don. Don headed for his sister, beckoning her away from the others.

"Daci? How is Payten?" He kept his eyes on Payten.

"She's hurting, Don. She doesn't understand why this has happened. She doesn't know who would do this. Payten is trying to work this through, to determine who it might be. And she can't."

"I see." Don paced for a moment, Daci waiting patiently for him to speak. "Paul's hurting, too."

"He is, Don." Daci turned as she heard footsteps. "Paul? What can we do for you?"

Paul shrugged, finding Payten searching for him. He walked towards his lady, just wrapping her in his arms. Payten felt safe with Paul. She just didn't understand why

"Payten? Are you okay?" Paul waited for her to speak, his arms tight around her.

Payten shrugged. She was not sure what to say. The caring of the ladies who had appeared helped to some extent. They were working around her garden, replanting what they could. Some were clearing away the debris from the swing. That saddened her, to see that destroyed. It had been her oasis when she needed that.

Chapter 20

Late that afternoon, Paul stood watching as Payten locked the front door. Her guests who now considered her a friend had left, making her promise to call them if she needed them or just needed to talk. He simply waited, knowing that she had felt overwhelmed for a while. This was not what she had been used to.

"Paul? Were that many people in my home?" Payten turned towards him, almost running into his arms.

"That many friends were. And Samuel and Aideen have more people that you can talk to. A detective friend. Their minister. And their police chief."

"Their police chief?" Payten could feel fear rising in her once more. *Please, Lord, can we end this and soon? I fear for Paul, that he will be seriously injured or even killed because of me.*

"Their police chief. Andrew. Andrew's wife, Phoebe, grew up thinking that Toryn was her cousin. Only he isn't. Theirs is quite the story."

"What is it with your friends? Can't they just do normal things?" Payten moved away from him towards her office. "What all did they find?"

"A lot of information. We'll need to go over it. But first, you need a break. You need to get away from here for a moment." Paul reached for her hand and then her keys. "Lock up, sweetheart. Let's go do something different and fun for a few hours."

———

"Something different and fun? And just what would that be?" Payten had to smile. She could not resist his infectious grin.

Paul shrugged. He wasn't sure what they could do. He just wanted to spend some time with her when she wasn't worried about something. Neither one saw the man who was leaning against the car parked down the road. Paul thought about it after and had nodded to himself. He had seen the man, stored his impression away in his brain, and remembered it when it was needed.

Ben watched as Paul seated Payten in a booth and then slid in beside her. He nodded, knowing that Paul had found his lady and was staking his claim as Ben would have put it. He walked over to slide onto the seat across from them, a grin on his face.

"Payten. Paul. What can we get for you two tonight?" His smile faded somewhat as he studied Paul. "Paul? Something has happened."

"It has. Payten's yard and gardens were destroyed and damaged early this morning. Thankfully, she didn't hear anything. But still, it has been devastating for her." Paul's hand reached for Payten's hand, stilling the restless movement of hers wiping at the table.

"It was? And you need help to clean it up?" Ben was ready to rise and go and help.

"No, it's all done. We had friends through today that helped. It's just hard for her to have her home invaded as it was." Paul's hand tightened on Payten's as she frowned at him. "That's what it was, Payten.

An invasion of your home and your life. We need to think through how to protect you."

Payten shook her head. It wasn't just her that needed protection. It was Paul. He needed someone to defend him as well.

"It's you too, Paul. Someone is after both of us. Only we don't know who or why." Payten shared a look with Ben, who was nodding. "You agree with me, right, Ben?"

"I do, unfortunately, Payten. I just don't know who would be after Paul. It could be anyone."

"That's what we think, Ben. And we can't narrow it down." Paul rubbed a finger at his temple. A headache was starting, a headache that he knew would only get worse with time.

"We'll need to think this through, Paul. There have been rumours on the street. That's worrying us."

"I'm sure that it is." Paul drew in a deep breath. He had to think this through and the headache was presently that.

Ben rose, heading for the kitchen and placing their food order. He stood where he could watch Paul and Payten. A movement at a nearby table caught his attention. Ben frowned. This was a stranger in town but he seemed too interested in Paul. He reached for his phone, snapping a photo of the man and then sending it on to Don. He knew that Don would reach out to his team and then to Aidan. He prayed that this would solve it for Paul.

Late that night, Payten curled up in bed. She had drawn the covers up as far as she could, feeling chilled. The situation this morning had scared her, almost terrorized her. She wanted this over. All she could do was pray for that to happen. Only, she didn't know that God was listening to her prayers. It didn't seem as if He was.

Payten slept at last. She didn't heard the tapping at her door and windows as someone tried to break in. She was overtired and that caused her to drop into a deep sleep. Her security system picked up the motion of the men. It just didn't pick up the faces. They were careful to keep them hidden.

Chapter 21

Paul walked towards their work van a week later. The team had been away on an assignment and was heading home. They were all exhausted. The protectee had fought them every hour of the days that they had been there. Don was seriously thinking that both Abe and Richard had the right idea. Training and staying in their home city to do so sounded better and better every time they turned to go home.

Sinking into his seat, Paul's eyes closed. He prayed for his lady, not having heard from her in the last couple of days. That worried him. He had had to set it aside and concentrate on what he was doing. Now, the worry resurfaced. Paul didn't see the looks that the others directed towards him. They all prayed for Paul and Payten, knowing that it was far from over for them.

Don reached for his phone, accessing his voice mail. His face grew stern as he listened to the call from Aidan. He sighed as he tucked his phone away. This voice mail message was not what he wanted to hear.

Thomas shot him a look from where he sat behind the driver's seat.

"Don?" His voice was low, only loud enough for Don to hear him. "You're troubled."

"I am." He turned his head to look at Paul, seeing that Paul had his eyes closed and his head back on the seat. "It was Aidan. It wasn't good news."

"Payten? She's okay?" Thomas really didn't expect Don to answer him before he spoke with Paul.

"Paul?" Don's voice roused Paul from the half-sleep that he had drifted into. "Aidan called."

"Payten?" Paul straightened up in his seat, his eyes not moving from Don.

"She's fine. Right now, Aidan has her safe in the department building. Her home was bombed this morning. Thank God that she was at work."

"How bad?" Paul's shared a look with his team, fear in his heart. All he could do was pray for his lady.

"It's destroyed, Paul. The fire department is still there." Don watched with compassion as Paul's eyes slid closed. "She's asked to move in with Daci for now. That works. Daci has good security."

"But it puts her at risk." Paul tried to think what he could do but his mind just couldn't take it in. This was his lady who was hurt and he wanted to make it all better.

"Daci knows that, Paul. She volunteered. It's going to be when Payten is out on her own that she's at most risk. We can't lock her away and throw the key in the garbage as much as we would like to." Don's mind was racing just as he knew that his team were working through this as well.

"Don? Did you mean it when you were muttering about doing training, similar to Abe and Richard?" Caleb asked the question that they had all wanted to ask.

"I am. I think that you guys want that as well." Don listened to the murmurs that filled the van. "We're home next week. We only have a couple more assignments on the books. We'll meet on Monday and start making plans. Richard will meet with us. He's already offered to." Richard and Don were lifelong friends, growing up in side-by-side homes.

"And Abe will too." Joshua nodded, having talked to Abe one day about what his team did now.

"I know he will. Think about it and put down your thoughts. Next week, we'll work on that and working on keeping Payten safe. I'll talk with Toryn and see what his feelings are. It is likely getting too dangerous for everyone around her."

"It is. We've talked about that, Don." Paul didn't elaborate. He just wanted to find his lady. His phone was out as he sent off a text message to her, not expecting the prompt response. A sad smile crossed his face. He wanted to hold her but they still had a number of miles to travel before he could do that.

Payten paced Aidan's office. He had stuck her away there, hoping to keep her safe. Aidan had a feeling that someone in the lab was responsible in some way for what was happening. He knew that feeling was like right. That disturbed him. Aidan had pulled the names of all the staff in the lab and was planning on working through a new investigation on them.

"Aidan? Is it someone who I work with?" Payten slumped into a chair, an action that was just not her. She kept her eyes on the floor, ashamed and embarrassed.

"It's possible, Aidan. We need to look at them." Aidan passed over the list. "Here. You work on giving me relatives for them, if you can."

"I can do some of them but not all. I don't work that closely with more than two or three. The others are more acquaintances." Payten's concentration centred on the list.

Aidan watched her for a moment, praying for her, before he was on his feet, seeing Toryn waiting just outside his door.

"Toryn?" Aidan swung his office door partly closed.

"Aidan? How is Payten?" Toryn was worried about her. Her house exploding as it had was not what had been expected.

"She's hurting, Toryn. She's worried that she's brought trouble into the lab. She's trying to come up with names of relatives for the teams there."

"That will help. It gives her a sense of being in control. Right now, she's not. That's never easy to take." Toryn rubbed at the back of his neck. "Don's heading this way once they hit town."

"I thought that they would be. Paul will want to be with her." Aidan paused, a thought crossing his mind.

"You think that Paul will marry Payten." Toryn's words were a statement, not a question.

"He might. I'm not sure that would be the right move." Aidan turned to watch Payten, finding her watching him in return.

"It might not be, but they might do that." Toryn walked away, puzzled at what was happening with Payten. They just didn't have enough information to understand it. He looked up to find the bomb squad leader waiting for him.

Chapter 22

Walking towards where Payten waited outside the police department that evening, Paul assessed his lady. She was stressed, he could tell just by how she was standing. He could feel the anger in her as well as he simply wrapped her into his arms.

Payten leaned against him, feeling safe and cherished at the same time. *Just how does that happen, Lord? It's strange to feel both of those emotions at once. Just let this end and soon. I fear for Paul's life.*

Payten leaned back, simply nodding at the question on Paul's face. Aidan approached them, a frown on his face.

"Paul? When did you get back?" Aidan stopped beside them. His eyes searched the area, knowing that someone was out there and watching them.

"Just about an hour ago. Don let me know what happened." Paul's arms did not let go of Payten. "We need to get her out of here."

"We do. Someone is out there, Paul, and watching you two very closely. Payten says that she's not getting the messages and packages that victims usually get." Aidan pointed to where Thomas and Mark were waiting. "You brought reinforcements."

"I did. Don, Joshua, and Caleb are here as well." Paul looked down at Payten, finding her watching him in return. "Come on, sweetheart. Let's get you to where you can be as safe as possible."

Payten simply nodded. She loved her work but during the last few days had felt unsafe there. She felt watched all the time. Aidan had listened to her and then cleared the lab to search it. His face had been grim as he approached her when he was done, holding up evidence bags of cameras and microphones near her work station. The concern, she knew, was that the evidence she had been working on had been compromised. She had agreed with Toryn that she needed to stay away and wait for whatever she was involved in to be resolved. Payten hated that.

Toryn had reached out to a neighbouring police department, asking for them to investigate. Bill Buckley, the lead detective from Elmton, had arrived a short while ago. He had brought one of his own teams with him. At the moment, he was locked in the lab with them, searching. It was going to be a long few days, Toryn knew, but necessary.

Paul headed for Thomas' truck. They had agreed that this was the route to go. Thomas and Mark would be in the front seat. Paul and Payten would be in the back seat. Daci was waiting at Don's home for them all. They had to make some decisions, and Daci had simply insisted that Payten needed another lady to weigh in on the decisions that would be made.

Payten stood for a moment, staring at Daci before she moved to hug her friend. She didn't know where she was heading. She was afraid, afraid that her friends would be hurt. Payten knew that she would be safe with them. She just didn't know their plans.

Don pointed towards the kitchen. He knew that Daci had been busy with their meal. They would eat and then spend time in prayer. All of his team was there. They would be at no other place given that it was one of their team involved.

Paul reached for Payten as they moved towards the office, their meal over and cleared away. His arm swept her close to him before he seated her in a chair and then sat at her feet. His eyes closed as their prayer time began. Paul felt the presence of God in the room. He knew the power of the prayers that his friends offered up.

Payten's arms wrapped around herself, her eyes focusing on Paul. She heard the prayers that were being uttered. She sensed Daci rising at one point and leaving the room.

Davi opened the door, allowing Aidan and another man who she didn't know to enter.

"Aidan? You're here?" Daci was hesitating for a moment.

"I am. This is Detective Bill Buckley. He needs to speak with Payten. She's here?" Aidan frowned at Daci as she didn't move.

"She is. They're involved in a time of prayer, Aidan. We can go on in." Daci turned, the two men following her. They stopped just inside the doorway, their heads bowing.

Don raised his head at last, frowning at Aidan and Bill before his eyes shifted to Payten. He found her watching Paul who in turn was watching Don. *This is crazy,* he thought. *We're watching one another watching one another and no one is ready to speak.*

"Payten?" Aidan waited patiently for Payten to look at him. "Payten, this is Detective Bill Buckley from Elmton. Toryn asked for their help in searching the lab. He needs to speak with you."

Payten was on her feet, moving away from Paul and towards the two detectives.

"Have you solved this yet?" Payten frowned at Aidan as he grinned at her.

"Not yet. But Bill does have some questions for you. Where can we meet?"

Payten shrugged before she headed for the kitchen.

"Here, I guess." She pulled out a chair, sat and then waited patiently for Bill to sit as well.

Bill assessed Payten as he set down his portfolio. Andrew McBeth, the Elmton chief, had asked him to investigate this incident. Not many people were aware that Andrew's wife, Phoebe, had been under the impression for many years that Toryn was a cousin of hers. Unfortunately, they had discovered that they were not related. That was a story in itself, one that he would share with this group if he needed to.

Chapter 23

Bill looked through his notes just to give Payten time to compose herself. He had deeper and harder questions for her. He knew that Aidan had asked some of them. Bill had Aidan's reports but needed to ask the same questions himself. It was what he did.

"Payten? Talk to me. Tell me about your family." Bill waited as he watched Payten blink.

"I lost them in a house fire. I ended up in foster care and hated every moment of it. It was not the life that I had led prior to that."

"The house fire? Was it an accident?" Bill watched her more closely, seeing the subtle shift in her expression.

"As far as I know that was what happened. I was told thought that it was arson. I never asked for the report. I was too devastated. Aidan said that he would look into it. I haven't heard what he found yet."

Bill nodded, knowing that Aidan had indeed looked into it and passed the paperwork on to him.

"It was an arson fire, Payten. You were not at home?"

"No, I was spending the night away with my class. I couldn't bear it at first. God is the only One that helped me." Payten blinked back tears. Her emotions were raw at this point.

"I understand. And they had no family?"

"Not that I know of. They never spoke of any. When I asked, they just said that they were all dead. I didn't understand that as a child and as I grew, I just shoved it aside. Maybe I shouldn't have. Is there a relative after me?" Payten buried her face in her hands for a moment, her emotions overcoming her.

"Not that I am aware of. We'll be looking into your family and your parents' families as well. Any friends that you had at the time. Your friends at present."

Bill waited patiently once more for Payten to look up.

"Payten? I need to talk to you about your friends as well."

"My friends? I don't have many. None of them are close. I keep to myself. It's all because of that assault in college. That destroyed something in me. I can't make friends very easily."

"That assault? Was the man ever arrested?" Bill looked down at Aidan's notes.

"Not that I know of. I know that Aidan has been looking into that."

"And I will as well. I need to do that, Payten, just to ensure that this is not related to what you are going through." Bill paused for a moment, rising to pour them a coffee and setting the mugs on the table before he sat once more. "Talk to me about your work."

Payten nodded, knowing that he would want as many details as she could give. She spoke quietly and calmly, not letting Bill read how she was actually feeling. That frustrated him. He needed to be able to read her emotions and just couldn't.

"Okay. I can understand what you do better now. Do you work on your own for the most part?"

"I do. We each are specialized in certain tests even though we can do most of the other testing that's required. It's how our lab works. Other than that, I don't know what to tell you." Payten wrapped her hands around her mug, needing to hold on to something. She just wanted Paul there to wrap her in his arms. That was the only place that she felt really safe, next to him.

"Now, for your other activities."

Payten gave him a list of what she normally did, a frown on her face as she concentrated. Only those activities would be changed, now that her home was gone. She said as much to Bill.

"I understand that, Payten. I'll be back and forth between here and Elmton over the next few days. I will have more questions for you."

Payten protested that, simply stating that she had told him everything that she could.

Bill's hand went up as he as Aidan hesitating in the doorway, not entering. "It's what we do, Payten. Aidan has been doing that. You know that it can be common practice to ask another force to investigate in something like this. I understand that you are off on leave for now."

"I am. I don't like it. I feel as if I am letting everyone down. And I don't know that I can go back to working there when this is over." Payten's head went down on the arms that she had folded on the table. "Do I have to leave the work that I love?"

"It's possible. We'll see what we can do about solving this right away. And then you can get back to work. I heard from Aidan that you are well liked there and everyone is pulling for you." Bill tucked away his pen, his hands folding on the table when he finished. "We're praying for you, Payten. That goes without saying."

"Thank you, Bill." Payten was on her feet, moving past Aidan who watched her almost run to where Paul was standing and waiting for her.

Paul wrapped her into his arms, turning her to the living room. He sat in the chair that he favoured and pulled her down on his knee. Payten's face was puzzled as he did that before she leaned back against him. She could hear conversation around them but was strangely content just to be held. She knew that God was in control and that He was defending her. She just wished that He'd hurry up and find the ones after her and Paul.

Don approached Bill, a hand out to shake the other man's.

"Toryn called Andrew."

"He did." Bill watched Payten. "It's what we do."

"We know. I'm glad that it's you. Maybe now we'll get some answers. Nothing against your teams, Aidan, but someone seems to be covering something up." Don was frustrated. "And I need to find some place to put her."

"That you do." Bill walked out with Aidan, their conversation quiet.

Aidan watched as Bill drove away before he studied the area around Don's house. His security was some of the best that he had seen. Somehow, though, it might not be enough. He knew that Payten would be out and about. She would not hide. And if she was, then Paul was going to be with her. Aidan frowned, a thought crossing his mind. How deeply did this involve Paul? It seemed that he was involved. Only Aidan had no idea how or why. All he could do was the petition God on behalf of his friends.

Chapter 24

Two days later, Payten sank to the back steps at Paul's house. He had found her earlier that morning and simply brought her to his house. She knew that some of his team mates had been around. Payten had heard Aidan's voice not long before and dreaded speaking with him.

Paul shook his head at Aidan's question. Aidan's question had not been unexpected. *No,* Paul thought to himself, *as much as I love Payten, it's not yet time to tell her. Why would Aidan ask that?*

"Paul, it is something to think about. You're in love. And it's obvious that Payten feels the most comfortable and safe with you. It's a natural step to take, you two getting married."

Paul was adamant that he would not. He wanted to court Payten, to use an old-fashioned term, and to do that when Payten was no longer in danger.

"Just think about it, Paul. It may come to that at some point." Aidan looked around. "Now, where is Payten? Bill is on his way to talk with her. He said that he had some information for her and more questions."

Sighing, Paul pointed towards the back door.

"She's out there. I want this over and over yesterday, Aidan."

"I know that, Paul, and we appreciate that. Now, let's find your lady and see what you have to say before Bill comes."

zPaul opened the back door, stepped through onto the back porch, and came to an abrupt stop. His hands were raised in the air.

Aidan stopped behind him, feeling something digging into his back. His eyes narrowed as he assessed the situation. His own hands raised in the air, he felt the tug as his police issue handcuffs was removed from their holster. He heard the back door open and close again before he was shoved forward.

Paul walked slowly towards where Payten was being held at gunpoint, her face angry. He sighed. *Lord, please calm my sweetheart. If she is this angry and tries something, one of us will be hurt or killed. I can't defend her if that happens to me. Aidan is with us. We'll find a way to escape at some point. For now, Lord, protect us all.*

Forced through the backyard of Paul's home and that of the neighbouring house backing onto his property, the trio were walked down the street and over many blocks to a house that stood on a large property, surrounded by a high fence. They were then forced through the gate and up the driveway and into the house. Payten whimpered for a moment as one of the men grasped her wrist in a tight hold and pulled her away from the men and shoved her down into a chair. A gun was shoved against her temple, a warning to the two men.

Paul and Aidan were forced into chairs on opposites walls, their glances confirming that they would try to escape when an opportunity arose. They were both committed to getting Payten away but at the moment, neither one would have an opportunity to do that.

Payten's heart pounded with fear not just for herself. She couldn't understand why they had been abducted or why Aidan was there, other than the fact that he had been with Paul. It was not a good scene, she decided. Her eyes searched the room, memorizing as much as she could of the room, its furnishings, and the men holding them. There were three men in the room with them, one of them standing beside each of the captives. The fourth man had disappeared.

Aidan's eyes narrowed as he too searched the room and then turned his attention to the men. He nodded to himself, thinking that he knew who they were. They were likely muscle for hire and all were likely wanted by not only his force. He sighed to himself before he too began to pray. Aidan knew that God was in control and had allowed this. He allowed both good and bad in His children's lives. All Aidan could do was pray for the three of them and that help would arrive shortly.

Paul's eyes were on Payten, watching her closely. He could see the fear and also anger in her. This was not how he had planned the day. He had expected Aidan and Bill to show up, go over what they needed to, and then Paul and Payten could get on with their day. To be walked away from his home at gunpoint had not been part of it.

Bill knocked loudly once more at Paul's front door. He frowned and then pulled out his phone. He nodded. This is where they were to meet. Aidan had confirmed that not even thirty minutes prior to Bill's arrival. Bill stepped backwards and then off the front porch to study the windows of the house. He had tried the front door, finding it locked. He walked around the house and back to the front porch, once more ringing the doorbell without any response.

Heading around to the back porch, Bill hesitated as he stepped up to the door. The knob turned under his hand before he frowned. This wasn't right, he thought.

"Hello? Paul? Are you here? Aidan?" Bill's voice echoed through the house. He entered, a hand on his weapon as he walked through the rooms, searching for anyone. He frowned once more. The house was empty. He searched outside and peeked through the garage windows. Paul, Payten, and Aidan were nowhere in sight, even though the vehicles belonging to both Paul and Aidan sat in the driveway.

Turning as he heard his name, Bill walked towards Don and Thomas as they stood on the driveway.

"Bill? You're here? But you're outside?" Don was puzzled at that.

"I am. There is no sign of Paul, Payten, or Aidan anywhere in the house or outside. They were to be here. Aidan had confirmed that he would be here."

Don's hand froze as he rubbed at his cheek. He nodded as Thomas reached for his phone and walked away, calling it in to the authorities.

An hour later, the three men stood quietly near Bill's car. Bill leaned against the driver's door, his arms folded across his chest. This was not how his day was to go. He had plans with his wife, Cora, and their young son, Michael, for later that day. It may well not happen, he thought, before he began to pray for his friends here in Oak City.

Toryn walked towards the three men, disturbed that two of his employees and friends had disappeared. There had been no sign of them at all. What puzzled them was the fact that Aidan's handcuffs was sitting on Paul's kitchen table. Aidan would not have willingly left them. They had been bagged as evidence before the team headed back tp the lab. They had promised to return Aidan's belongings to Toryn as soon as they were finished with their investigation of them.

Chapter 25

Toryn stopped beside the three men, Don reading his face. There was no sign of the three. And that was concerning. It was not like any of them to disappear if they knew someone was expected there.

"I have the bomb squad coming through, Don. Just as a precaution." Toryn waited for a moment. "Bill? You're here? You were through the house."

"I was, Toryn. I was. I couldn't get an answer when I knocked. The back door was unlocked. When I didn't get an answer, I walked through just to ensure that they weren't there." Bill was frustrated at not finding the ones who he needed to speak with.

"About what I figured you would. It's a step that we would have taken."

Bill rubbed at his cheek. "I need to get back to Elmton soon but I don't want to leave if you need me."

"You've given your statement?" At Bill's nod, Toryn shrugged. "We can call you back if we need to. I suspect that we will. For now, hand over what you can give me and then head home. I'll call you later this afternoon or this evening just to let you know what is happening and if they have shown up." Toryn watched Bill carefully before he motioned him away from the other two men. "Bill? What can you tell me?"

"What can I tell you? Payten is in deep danger. I left information for you with your desk officer. There is a leak in your lab and that leak has endangered Payten. And through Payten, they are going after Paul.

———

The information that we've uncovered is that for some reason, they connected the pair. And we feel that Don may be an indirect target. It was that way with Richard."

"I know. Richard and Don are good friends, as I'm sure you know. He'll head this way as soon as he hears." Toryn paused his words, turning as he heard footsteps. "And there is Richard and Stephen."

"I thought Richard would head this way. He called me last night, concerned about Don. I couldn't say much but I didn't need to. Don has been in touch with him, I gather."

"They would be. Head off, Bill. And thank you. I'll go over what you've left. I'll call you with my questions. Just pray that these three are not hurt and will be home safely in the next few hours."

"It's how we always pray, Toryn. But it isn't always how God answers." Bill walked away, heading for his car. He noted that Don and Thomas had headed for the new arrivals. He waved as he opened his car door.

Richard looked around as Bill drove away and then turned back to Don.

"Don? What can we do for you? My team is worried about you and your team."

Don nodded, knowing that was in fact true. He had been like that when Richard's team had gone through what they had not that long ago.

"We get that, Richard. We've been friends for too long to hide anything from one another. Now, we need to work through this. I'll lock up Paul's home and then head for mine. I see that Thomas and Stephen have already left."

"They have. Stephen was muttering something as we parked but he didn't elaborate on it. Something about an address that he had come across."

"Our team has taken up the search. You know that they will. And Emma is on board. I was talking with Abe last night and he was asking about you. Something told him that you were in trouble."

"I don't understand how Abe knows other than God. He has been used so many times in the past."

"He has been. Now, where's your truck?"

The men walked towards Don's truck, not seeing the man watching from the neighbouring property. The man nodded. Paul had friends working to find him. He knew where Paul was being held. He just had to determine which friend of Paul's to approach. Don was not his first choice.

Mark, Joshua, and Caleb turned as they heard Don's truck, moving towards Don and Richard.

"What happened, Don?" Mark spoke for the trio.

"Paul, Payten, and Aidan are missing. They disappeared from Paul's home. Bill discovered that fact when he appeared at Paul's home." Don unlocked his home, heading for the office. "Put on the coffee, Caleb. We're going to need a lot of it, I suspect."

"That's about what I thought." Caleb had already headed that way, Joshua working with him.

Richard paced Don's office, his hands jammed into his jeans. He had no idea what his friend was facing. He didn't think that Don did either.

"Don, talk to me. Tell me what all has happened. We have spoken to some extent but there is more to what you've said."

"There is. And I'm not sure that we can even explain it." Don sat at his desk, reaching for the folders that he had stacked there the night before.

"Explain what you can. I'll take notes." Richard's phone was out as he heard a chime. "Emma's sending you information as well as to me."

Don nodded, pulling up his email program. He opened Emma's email, reading what she had sent him and then printing off copies. Mark was there, to collate them for him.

"Richard, we need to pray for our friends. I fear for them. And only God can protect them and defend them."

"That is too true." Richard accepted his mug of coffee as he found somewhere to spt. He studied all the men with him and then raised his eyes as Daci appeared.

Daci had been worried about Payten since she had left that morning.

"Don? Where're Paul and Payten?" Daci moved quickly into her brother's hug, sensing that he had bad news.

"They've disappeared, Daci. And so has Aidan. All from Paul's home. Bill found that out when he showed up."

"Disappeared? Oh, no! I was afraid of that!" Daci spun to stare at the men, seeing the concern on their faces that not one of them was trying to hide.

"We'll find them, Daci." Caleb spoke up. "And we will bring them home. God's not done with them yet."

Chapter 26

Don rose at last, heading for the kitchen, Daci on his heels. It was nearing a mealtime and while none of them felt like eating, it was necessary.

"Where are they, Don?" Daci worked away on sandwiches as Don worked on another aspect of their meal.

"I don't know, Daci. I wish that I did. I would go and bring them home." Don paused, his hand hovering over the cookie tin for a moment before he reached into it.

"So would I. Any of these guys would." Daci wiped her hands on a towel, throwing it on the granite counter before she headed for the door. She stood back as she saw Toryn waiting there with another man who she did not recognize. "Toryn?"

"Daci. How are you today?" Toryn gave her a quick hug before he moved past her into the hallway. "This is a friend of mine from Riverville. Frankie Brennan. He's another detective friend."

"I see. Welcome, Frankie. We're just ready to take a break for lunch. You are both welcome to join us."

Frankie nodded as Toryn glanced at him.

"That would be welcome. Thank you, Daci." Frankie hesitated a moment, not sure where to head.

"They're in the office, Toryn. Go on through." Daci returned to the kitchen, not seeing that both

Frankie and Toryn had followed her until she heard Don greeting them both. She frowned at them.

Toryn and Frankie reached to help with the trays, their conversation quiet with Don before they headed for the office. The two newcomers greeted Richard as he headed for Daci.

"Daci? What else do we need?" Richard reached for the tray that Daci was just reaching for. "Here. Let me."

"I think that we have everything, Richard. Thank you." Daci paused, her eyes on their friend. She had known Richard all her life and was so glad that he had a lady to love in his life. "What would you do, Richard?"

"To find them?" At Daci's nod, Richard set the tray back on the table. He reached to hug her before he began to pace. "That's what Don has asked. I am not sure what I would do. I know what we did when one of our team disappeared. This is different, though, with an officer missing. The officers on the force will be out there looking for him, whether they are on duty or on their own time. They will head for the streets as well. "

"That's what I thought. But there should be something that we can do." She stared at him. "Tracking."

Richard grinned at her before pointing a finger at her.

"Bingo! I asked a friend to bring in a dog. He and his wife are doing that. He's an officer on a nearby county force. His wife works search and rescue in her spare time from being a physician. They would be there just around dusk. That can't be helped."

"No, that's fine. I pray that they will find them and soon." Daci walked away, heading for the bedroom that Don had designated as hers. She sank to the side of the bed, her head bowing as she prayed.

Don came looking for her, pausing at her doorway, before he walked away. Richard had simply said that he was concerned about Daci before Don nodded and headed after her. He returned to sit at his desk, his eyes on his friends.

Richard looked towards Frankie, a frown appearing for a moment. He wasn't sure why Frankie had appeared and with Toryn. There was something up and that he prayed was good news.

"Frankie?" Don waited for Frankie to look at him. "Are you here as an officer or a friend?"

"A friend, Don. Just as a friend. I was speaking with Bill earlier today and then Abe approached me. He's not able to make it here and asked if I would represent him."

"Abe did? Then, he's weighing in." Don shared a look with Richard. It was not the first time that Abe had done something like that. "Okay, so, what has Emma come up with?"

Frankie began to laugh, knowing that Don had gone right to why he was there. He held up a folder.

"This. She's been working through Paul and Payten's families and friends, including you all. She has information that she needs to confirm with both Paul and Payten. She's been looking for them. When I spoke to Bill earlier, he simply said that Paul and Payten were missing. Emma sent me with the information." Frankie handed over the folder. "She's kept back what she needs to confirm. This is what she has confirmed."

"That's fine. Hopefully, we'll have them home in the next few hours." Don sorted through the paperwork, handing it off to Joshua and Caleb who had risen to take it. Copies were made and passed out to all of the ones present.

Daci curled up in a chair, a cup of tea in her hand, watching the men working away. They all worked together well, she thought, even Frankie.

Toryn read through the paperwork and then read through it again. *Emma's good,* he thought. *I wonder how she does this. And I know that she can't explain it. But where do we go with this? I need Aidan here to work on this and he's not.* His phone chiming had him setting aside the paperwork and rising to walk away and take his call.

"Tad? What have you and Suzy found?" Toryn stopped in the kitchen, reaching for a pad of paper and a pen. "Where did the trail end? I see. No, I don't know that we have enough information to get a search warrant. And we have no guarantees that they are still there."

"It looks as if the trail ends at the gate. Beauty is quite certain that they were walked through there. They did walk them for quite a few blocks, though. I don't understand walking them and not shoving them into a vehicle." Tad was puzzling through his thoughts.

"It is strange, Tad. I appreciate you and Susy taking time on a Saturday to do this. Call me on Monday and I'll update you on what we have." Toryn tucked away his phone, his thoughts troubled. He knew that address. It belonged to someone high in the city industry. He could not see him being involved, but stranger things had happened over time.

Chapter 27

Payten glared at the man standing beside her. He had holstered his weapon but didn't move from standing next to her. That bothered her. She wanted to run and couldn't. Her eyes moved to Paul, finding him not moving except for his eyes, which were in constant motion. She next moved her gaze to Aidan, finding him watching her before he gave a faint nod.

Aidan was puzzled. This was not what he had expected. They had been brought into that house, made to sit, and then left as they were. This just didn't happen. They were waiting for someone to come in. He just prayed that it would be a friend and not someone who would mean them harm.

Paul was puzzled as well. This was not how things worked. He was only too familiar with hostage situations. And that was what he felt they were. Hostages at the hand of someone who didn't want to appear. He switched his gaze to Aidan and then to Payten. He tried to signal to her that he would protect her but wasn't sure if she could read what he was attempting to tell her.

Having had enough, Payten jumped to her feet and began to pace, the man guarding her just watching and not making her sit back down. Aidan and Paul both frowned at this. This was unexpected, to say the least. Paul prayed that Payten was not making a mistake by doing what she had.

Aidan watched the men closer. He frowned. There was something going on here. He didn't think that they meant them harm but kidnapping a police officer would bring severe consequences.

Hearing voices approaching the room, Payten spun, her eyes on the closed door. *This is it, isn't it, Lord? This is where we live or die. Please let Paul and Aidan live. I don't care about myself.*

The door swung open as a man shoved at it. He pushed at the wheels on his chair, stopping just inside the door. His keen eyes studied each of the three, a frown on his face as he saw Payten on her feet.

"Sit, young lady. We need to talk, all four of us. My men will leave. Once we've spoken, then I'll see that you get home."

"This is kidnapping, Judge. You do know that?" Payten was not backing down. "And you kidnapped a police officer too."

"I know. It is not something that I did lightly. Aidan, I apologize for my man's taking of your handcuffs." The judge's gaze went to Paul next. "Paul, I apologize to you as well. I watched you grow over the years. I knew your father well. He was a friend of mine. I was ready to reach out to you just as you graduated high school. I lost track of you at that point."

"Judge Greer? Dad spoke of you over the years. I would not have expected you to take these steps." Paul was not backing down from his father's former friend.

"No, I shouldn't have. But you are being watched and watched closely. I took a chance on finding you and Payten. Aidan, I need you to listen closely to what I have to say. You have your phone. Send out a text to Toryn and explain to him that you are with me, if he doesn't know that already. I am told that a couple and a Border collie were seen outside of the gate. I suspect that it was Tad and Suzy with her Beauty."

Aidan nodded, before his phone was out, sending off a message to Toryn that he, Paul, and Payten were safe and that he would explain as soon as he could. He added that Judge Greer had wanted to speak with the couple but had not felt free to approach them.

Toryn read the text before he sighed and then nodded. This was not what he had expected to read. Judge Greer was a highly respected officer of the court. He had no idea what consequences he would face. He would need to reach out to the judge.

Don watched Toryn carefully before he approached him. Toryn nodded towards the front door. Once outside, he simply handed Don his phone. Reading it, Don blinked, not sure that he had read the text correctly.

"Judge Greer?" Don was shocked, to say the least.

"Judge Greer. I'm heading that way. Stay and work on what Emma sent. I'll bring them all here. And that will be tonight." Toryn walked away, Don watching him do that before he turned back to the house.

Judge Greer waited, knowing that the three had questions for him. He also knew that Toryn would arrive shortly and he wanted Toryn there when he spoke.

Toryn paused just outside of the living room door in the judge's home. He saw Payten as she perched on the edge of her chair.

"Chief? I apologize for this." Judge Greer spun his chair to face Toryn. "I will accept any repercussions that come. But I do need to speak with these three young people. They are all watched very carefully and I did not feel that I could approach them without bringing them here."

"I see, Judge Greer. There may be repercussions. For now, we talk. What is it that you needed to speak with these three about?" Toryn found a chair, sat, and then waited patiently.

Judge Greer nodded, knowing that Toryn would weigh his findings and what the judge had to say.

"Thank you for that, Toryn. You have always been a fair man. Now, this young man, Paul? His father and I were good friends when we were younger. There is something in Paul's background that Paul not likely knows about." Judge Greer peered at Paul. "Paul, you are a good man, just like your father. He was a good friend to me. We spent many hours studying God's word together and in prayer. Your mother was a good friend to my wife." Judge Greer paused for a moment, watching Paul closely.

"I remember you, Judge. You spent many hours in our home. I have memories of you and your wife. Dad spoke of you many times as well." Paul swallowed hard, trying to control his emotions. He missed his parents, just needing them there for this. They weren't. *God, is this You? Are you bringing someone back into my life that knew them, that can help me to understand what happened?* "Thank you, Judge. I wish that you had just asked me to come and see you. I would have. So would Payten and Aidan. I pray that your actions do not have consequences for you."

"I am retired now, Paul, and not practicing. So if you're worried about the law society, don't be. Aidan? I have followed you as well. Let's talk and then my men have prepared a meal for us. I would ask that you join me for that. If you choose not to, then I accept that."

Chapter 28

Judge Greer once more studied the three young people sitting in front of him. He smothered a smile as Payten finally sat back, a frown on her face. She was troubled, he could tell, and not just from this. He had watched her over their years at church and had kept track of her work habits. He had been about to approach her to come and work for him in his investigation firm when all this had broken loose. He knew that Paul was happy and content with where he was and what he was doing. It had been Paul's desire since he was young to be in law enforcement of some kind. His father had not dissuaded him from that.

"Toryn, before we start, will you pray for this? We need that. These three young people are in danger and that is closing in on them. Aidan, you are in danger just because you are friends with them and also because you are the investigator on this case." Judge Greer's eyes closed as Toryn prayed. He was not surprised to hear the two younger men pick up the petition but somewhat surprised with Payten did. His own prayer closed that time.

Judge Greer sat for a few moments, his head bowed and his eyes still closed. He was waiting for word from the Lord before he spoke. He nodded at last, his head raising, his eyes locking with those of Paul.

"Paul, I am sorry that you ended up in foster care. I wanted to take you in but Belle was so sick at the time and I didn't feel that I could. Your parents had no relatives to step forward to take you in, as I am sure that you are aware.”

Paul nodded, unable to speak for a moment. He felt a hand on his and realized that Payten had simply picked up her chair, set it down beside him, and reached for his hand to comfort him. His grip tightened on her hand.

“I always wanted someone to step in. I just knew that there was no one.” Paul drew in a deep breath, trying to control his emotions.

“We understand that, Paul. We looked for someone for you but could find no one. That troubled us.” Judge Greer shared another look with Toryn, who simply shook his head.

Toryn listened to Judge Greer speak to Paul, his thoughts troubled for his friend. Who was after Paul? And then again, who was after Payten? That was a question that they were all struggling to understand. Not one of them had come close to an answer for either question.

“I don’t get it, Judge. Why me?” Paul’s hand tightened its grip once more on Payten’s hand.

“That is something we’re working hard to discover. I have information that I will pass on to both you and Aidan. It has been confirmed through my sources. There is a group here in town that is after you and your team, Paul. We’ve seen that before in other teams. We don’t know who all is involved as yet. That we will continue to work on.” The judge’s gaze turned to Payten. “As for you, young lady, what do we tell you?”

Payten shrugged, not sure what was going on or who to trust any more.

"That this is over? I just want to go home. Only I have no home any more. Someone destroyed it and any memories that I had." They could hear the devastation in her voice even as she struggled to hold back her tears.

"That they did, Payten. I'm sorry for that. I have a home that you can use, if you wish. It has very good security on it and it is right next to Paul's." Judge Greer grinned at Paul. "Didn't know that, did you?"

"No, sir. I didn't. I knew that it has had tenants on occasion but I just never thought much about it."

"No, you won't. You live a peaceful life at home, Paul, when you are there. Aidan? I'm sorry to involve you like this, but you need to be. I trust you bear no hard feelings?" The judge knew Aidan's character. He too had been followed by the judge.

"No, sir. I just wish that you had asked us. We would have come willingly. Now we have to explain to my fellow officers what happened."

"We'll do that, Aidan." Toryn spoke up at last. "I'll take care of it. Judge, no more of this. You want to speak with us, you call me."

"I will, Toryn. Now, I have a meal ready for you. Or if you wish you can leave. You are free to do so."

The four exchanged glances before they nodded. They would grant him that meal but then leave.

Paul pulled out his phone, walking away to a corner of the room. He sent off a quick text to Don, who responded rapidly, simply asking if he was okay and where he was.

Payten moved to stand beside him, his arm coming out to wrap around her.

"Okay, sweetheart?" Paul kept his voice low.

"I think so. I just don't understand this. He has not explained very well why he had us brought here."

"No, he hasn't." Paul watched the judge carefully, still not sure what was going on. "I don't know that I can trust him now. This is still too strange."

"It is. I don't know about eating with him. I guess that's okay." Payten walked towards the dining room, her hand tight in Paul's.

Toryn watched the couple carefully, seeing their uneasiness. It echoed his. Aidan moved up beside him.

"Do you trust him. Toryn?" Aidan kept his voice low.

"I'm not sure, Aidan. I'll have Emma look into him. There is something off about all of this."

"There is. And I think we need to look deeply into him. For now, do we trust his meal?"

Toryn shrugged, not quite sure if they could or not. They didn't have much choice, he decided, at the present time. He knew that he would be eating very lightly and suspected the other three would be as well.

Chapter 29

Standing on his paved driveway an hour later, Don watched closely as Paul stalked towards him, Payten's hand tight in Paul's. He could tell that they were upset and almost angry. He didn't think that he had seen Paul in quite that state of emotions.

"Paul?" Don waited for Paul to stop beside him. He knew that Thomas had stayed, the other three men having commitments that they could not avoid.

"Don? Who all is still here?" Paul stopped beside his team leader.

"Thomas is. He stayed just to assess you two. The others had to leave." Don pointed towards the house. "Inside with the both of you." He watched the area around his home, feeling them being watched. Whoever it was? They were staying close enough to monitor the team's activities.

Paul nodded, walking towards the porch where Thomas was waiting for them. He gave an abrupt nod, tugging Payten into the house, finding Daci waiting for them. Daci simply hugged them and then with an arm around Payten, simply led her to a bedroom where she pointed to the clean clothes that she had set out.

Payten rubbed at her wet hair when she had finished her shower and dressed once more. She felt somewhat better but she was worried and also troubled by the adventure that they had just undergone. She paused, her eyes closing as she struggled to control her tears. She prayed, petitioning God for protection for

Paul and also that this, whatever this was, would be over and soon.

Paul looked up from where he was leaning against a wall as her door opened. He too had cleaned up, feeling refreshed to some degree. He saw the woebegone look on her face and simply opened his arms. Payten fled across the hall to him, to be wrapped tightly in his arms. Paul's prayer for his lady intensified. He knew that he had fallen in love with Payten and wanted no other lady to share his life. He just didn't know how Payten was feeling towards him. They would need to speak with one another.

"Okay, sweetheart?" Paul's voice was low in Payten's ears, stilling her movements.

Payten leaned back a bit to stare up at Paul. It was not the first time that he had called her that. She saw the look in his eyes and her face softened.

"Paul? Is that what I am?"

"What? I don't understand?" Paul's words had been automatic. He had not realized that he had been calling her sweetheart.

"Am I your sweetheart?" Payten waited.

Paul's face contorted for a moment with his emotions before he nodded.

"You are. And you have been for a while." Paul dropped a kiss on her forehead. "We'll talk, sweetheart. But right now? Let's find the others. Thomas, our paramedic, wants to check us over, just to be safe and to have a record on file with Don. Then, we'll talk with Don and Daci. Thomas is off soon to travel out of town for the next week."

"He stayed?" Payten was not used to that. Her friends would just have left. She frowned as she wondered at her friends and just how much of friends that they were.

"He did. It's what we do for one another, Payten. We're friends, team mates, and almost brothers. Our work has done that." Paul reached for her hand, heading for Don's office, knowing that was where the other three would have gathered.

Daci listened carefully to what the pair were saying. She nodded. She had heard rumours about Judge Greer, some good and others not so good. She saw the tension in Payten and sighed. *This is not going so well, is it, Lord? How do we help her? I can help her from my standpoint, but someone else needs to talk to her. She is a victim, just as Paul is. Who can I reach out to?*

Don shifted on his chair, his eyes on Paul. Paul was staring back at him. Don nodded. Something was troubling Paul and he would dig until he found out what it was.

"Paul? What happened? How did you end up at Judge Greer's?" Thomas had decided not to leave, feeling that this was more important.

"I have no idea. We were taken from my yard and walked to his home. It was a good dozen blocks or more. We were then sat down in his living room. We waited for a while before the judge appeared. Toryn showed up not too much later. The judge never said what he wanted. It was almost as if it was a fishing expedition on his part." Paul looked towards Payten, seeing her nodding.

"He said that he was friends with your parents and had wanted to take you in. He could have. He didn't. Some of what he said just didn't make any sense." Payten laid her hand on Paul's arm, finding his other hand covering her.

"No, it didn't make sense. And I think you're right. He was on a fishing expedition. I know that Aidan will be looking into him closely. And I think that we need to involve Emma."

"She's involved, Paul." Don reached for some paperwork. "After Toryn left, I reached out to her. She has sent on some information for us. I would suggest, though, that we set it aside for the night and take it up in the morning when we're fresh."

The pair agreed with Don and conversation became more general. Paul's arm went around Payten without either of them noticing as he tucked her closer to him. Daci and Thomas shared a look and a smile. Their friend was falling in love and doing that in front of them.

Don walked around his house near midnight, searching for anything that shouldn't be there. He paused near the back of his yard, sending someone waiting. He was not wrong. A youth from the streets was there, handing over a package. He was gone before Don could question him. Don stared down at the package and sighed. This was changing things, he thought. He headed for his house and his bed, but not to sleep. Instead, he spent the night in intercessory prayer for his friends.

Chapter 30

Paul was on his feet in the early morning hours, hearing Payten muttering to herself outside of his door. He opened it to find her standing and staring at it, her arms wrapped around herself. He simply swept her into a hug and then turned her towards the kitchen. Seating her, he sat beside her, his hands reaching for hers.

"Payten? You're awake really early." Paul waited patiently for Payten to speak, his heart raising in prayer for his lady. "You're troubled."

"I am, Paul I can't stay with Don or Daci for that long. I need to find my own place. Only it's not there any more. What am I to do?" Payten blinked rapidly in an attempt to control her tears.

Paul sighed. This was not how he had planned this day. Don would be up soon, he decided, as he squinted at the clock on the stove. He wanted to talk with Payten about where they went in their relationship. That he could not and would not do in front of Don.

"Payten? Let's head over to Ben's for breakfast. I know it's early, but he'll be there already. We can eat breakfast with Ben or Rachel and then talk."

Payten studied him, feeling safe with him and knowing that he would do his best to protect her. That was who he was and what he did. She shrugged, on her feet and headed for the closet where she had hung her jacket the night before. Paul was on her heels, a note left on the kitchen table for Don. Don had taken Paul to his own home the evening before so that Paul could retrieve his truck.

Ben watched the couple as Paul entered through the back door, waving as he did so. Paul then headed for Ben's office despite the protest that Payten offered. Ben shook his head. They were in love with one another, just not willing yet, he didn't think, to acknowledge it.

"Paul? You're here early." Ben followed them, pointing to the chairs and a small table in the corner of the room. "I heard about yesterday."

"We are. And you did? How?" Paul sat near Payten, his hand reaching for hers.

"Word is on the street. How far do you trust the judge?" Ben sat as well, waving at the cook who had peeked in the door. The cook simply nodded and walked away. The breakfasts would be in soon, Ben knew.

"I'm not sure. It was just so bizarre, Ben. He could have asked us to come. Instead, he had his men walk us there. One of them did hold a weapon on Payten. And to force Aidan to come too. That's going to take some explaining. Toryn did show up."

"I know that he did. You two are being watched by two different parties. One means you harm. The other doesn't. That group? They are watching out for you."

"And we appreciate that." Payten spoke at last. "How well do you know the judge?"

Ben shrugged He was not sure what to say to that. He knew of the judge and his involvement in trying to clean up their town. This time? He had not taken a very smart way to do that and could face consequences because of how he had approached Paul and Payten, involving Aidan as he had. Ben worked closely with him, both men concerned about Paul and Payten now.

"Well enough, I guess." Ben waited as their meals were set down in front of them "We need to talk more at some point, Paul. I suspect that is why you came."

"Not really, Ben. I'm not sure why I came here Other than for a meal." Paul grinned at his friend. "But you're right. There is an undercurrent here in town that has grown worse over the years. My team has talked about it. How do we stop what is going on?"

"That is a good question, Paul. I am not sure that we can at this point. And I fear that whoever is behind this will go after each one of your team members. It's what has been done in other areas."

"It has. Richard and Abe both went through that with their teams." Paul bite into the whole wheat toast that he favoured, his eyes on Payten as she stared down at her food. "Payten? What are your thoughts?"

"I think that Ben is correct. There has been an undercurrent here in town. I just don't know that we can solve this without someone being seriously hurt or even killed." Payten blinked for a moment, her thoughts muddled. That was not like her, she knew.

Her thoughts were usually very organized. It just seemed that being near Paul changed that.

"What have you heard over the years, Payten?" Ben prodded her gently, letting her take time to compose her thoughts. "And eat your breakfast. It's not so good when it goes cold." He simply grinned at her frown.

"Thank you, Ben. I appreciate the meal. There is just too much going on right now. Where is God in all this?" Payten asked that question, not really expecting an answer. She didn't hear the footsteps that had approached and jumped as she saw their minister sitting down with them. She frowned at him in turn.

Gideon Howe grinned at the trio. He had felt led by God to find Ben that morning, not knowing that he would also find Paul and Payten. That was a couple who he wanted to speak with. He just had not been able to track them down together to do so. God had laid them on his heart in a way that he usually didn't feel such a burden.

"Gideon? What can you tell us about this?" Ben nodded towards the couple.

"What can I tell you? Where is God in this?" Gideon kept his eyes on Payten, seeing Paul nodding as he listened to the questions.

"Yes, Gideon, where is God? I feel as if He's not here any more. I know in my heart that He is in charge of the situation, that He will defend us in whatever we face. It's hard to trust." Payten was not sure that she was expressing herself properly.

"It's normal to ask those questions, Payten. We're human. We need answers that may take a while to come. God expects that of us. He doesn't stop loving us or protecting us. You know that, I know from other conversations that we have had over the years. Now, as to what you and Paul are facing as a couple? That's more difficult to explain. God is there with both of you. He promises never to leave you or forsake you. He covers you in the hollow of the rock with His hand. Remember as well that Christ prayed for you in the garden. I take great comfort in that fact. It has gotten me through many difficult situations." Gideon paused for a moment, his eyes shifting to Paul, finding Paul watching Payten intently. "Paul? I know that you are doing your best to protect Payten. Unfortunately, you can't be with her all the time. Your team is away for days at a time on your assignments. Payten? Are you working right now?"

"No. I was asked to take a leave of absence. I agreed that I am not safe to be at work. And there are issues there as well." She blew out a breath. "To tell you the truth, Gideon? I don't know what to do. I can't sit idle but I feel that if I am around people, I bring them danger."

"Yes, there is that. Tell you what. I have a friend who needs someone just to be with them during the day when their family is away. You know her very well. It's Elise Watkins. She has good security at her home. She has asked about you, worried that you are alone. In fact, she has asked me if you would like to move in with her, given what happened to your home."

Payten stared at him, her mouth snapping closed as Paul tapped at her chin. This was not what she had expected.

Chapter 31

Paul approached his team later that day. He was frustrated, to say the least. He had seen the car that had been following him. He had run towards it but it had taken off, leaving dust in its wake. He knew that God was protecting him and defending him against his enemies, but he still wanted this over. It was not that Paul didn't place his trust in God. It was just that he wanted to date Payten and couldn't or wouldn't while they were in danger.

Thomas watched him closely, assessing him as best that he could. He shook his head. Paul was under a lot of stress, Thomas knew, but he had the support of all of the team.

"Paul?" Joshua frowned at him. "What was that all about?"

"That? That car was tailing me. I couldn't get the plate number to see who it is. Not that it likely would have mattered."

"Not likely." Caleb spoke up. "It is probably stolen."

The men walked towards the office building, knowing that Don had called a meeting for them all. It was an unusual move for him to call a meeting on short notice.

Don watched as the men found their seats at the conference table. He studied Paul the hardest, seeing the subtle signs that he was under stress. He was not happy with what was happening with Paul but they couldn't avoid it.

"Let's pray, friends. Then, I have some thoughts to run by you."

Their heads raised at last, the men exchanged glances. Don had walked out of the room for a moment. They didn't see him standing in the hallway, assessing each one of them before he nodded. He walked back into the room, returning to his seat at the table. He didn't speak for a moment, his fingers tapping at the folder in front of him. Don seemed to make a decision. He opened the folder and then passed around the papers. The men looked at them and then at Don.

"Read through this, men. Then, we'll talk."

The men were quiet as they read through the documents. Caleb raised his head at last, exchanging a glance with Joshua before they both looked at Don.

"Don? What is this?" Mark spoke for the group.

"This? We've talked about this. We don't want to travel forever. We've seen how Abe and Richard have transitioned to training. It's something that I think we should look into. Paul is wanting to date Payten. I know that each of us wants that for ourselves. We want a lady and a family of our own. Just when that happens? It's in God's hands. But I think that we should plan that way, that we no longer travel. We can pick up enough day work here in the area as well as training to some extent. We'll pray about it. When the time is right, we'll talk to both Abe and Richard."

Paul rose at last, tapping the papers neatly back into the folder. He was anxious to find Payten but just felt that he had to wait. Don eyed him closely before he approached him.

"Paul? You're not leaving? Everyone else has." Don frowned as Paul shook his head.

"I can't, Don. I just can't. God won't let me." Paul paced, frustration evident on his face but also confidence in his trust in God. "Someone is out there."

Don nodded. That sense of someone meaning them harm had saved them in their work many times. Even in their personal life, they trusted their instincts, knowing that God was protecting and defending them. He walked away and pulled out his phone.

"Aidan? Where are you?"

"Coming up to your place." Aidan suddenly threw his phone to the seat, cutting off Don's voice. His car in park, he was out of it and running towards the youth standing near Don's driveway. Tackling the youth, Aidan drew him to his feet and handcuffed him.

"Talk, man. Why are you here?" Aidan's hand on the youth's arm shoved him towards the car where he was in turn shoved inside. Aidan shook his head. This was not what he had expected. Opening the front door, he retrieved his phone, calling for help.

"Don?" Aidan's voice echoed across the airwaves to Don. "Stay inside. I just arrested someone outside the building."

"You did? Paul felt that he couldn't leave. This has to be why. Come find us when you can." Don pocketed his phone, turning to Paul.

"Someone was out there?" Paul slumped back against the table. "Did the others not see him?"

Don shrugged. He was not aware that they had. He knew his men well enough that if they had, they would have held onto the youth until the authorities arrived.

Paul shared a look with Don before he walked away. Aidan watched him do that before he shook his head.

"I wanted to talk with him, you know."

Don began to laugh, bringing a wry grin to Aidan's face.

"I know. He knows that too. Catch up with him later. I can guarantee you that he's gone to find Payten, wherever she is. And he'll know that." Don locked up the building and then walked towards his house, Aidan keeping step with him. "Who was it?"

"A youth. I'm not sure who he is. We'll investigate him, that's a given." Aidan paused, rubbing at his cheek. "How is Paul? I can't get him to a straight answer from him."

"And you won't. Not at present. He's not sure himself. We've talked. I've sent him to Richard's team and Abe's team to talk with them. That's helping, he said. It's this with Payten. He wants to date her but doesn't think that she would want to at this point, not when they're both in danger."

———

159

Aidan shrugged, his thoughts going back to his conversations with Payten.

"Somehow, I don't think that would matter to Payten. She feels safe with Paul. And they both need that right now. Listen. I have to run. I'm due for a conversation with someone shortly. Call me if you need me." Aidan walked away rapidly, leaving Don staring after him.

Chapter 32

Payten looked around as she heard footsteps on the dark oak floor. A huge smile lit up her face as she moved into Paul's hug. She clung to him for a moment, fear rising inside her. She just knew that they were still in danger and just when that danger would rear its ugly head was an unknown.

"Paul? You're done for the day?" Payten leaned back to stare up at him, wonder in her heart that she had found such a tall boyfriend.

"I am. I had to find you." Paul hugged her tight again before turning her to the outdoors and the seats on Don's back deck. Daci and Payten were still with Don, despite Payten's protest that she should be somewhere else.

"Paul? What happened?" Payten snuggled down in Paul's arms as they sat on the swing on the porch.

"Someone was waiting for me outside of Don's building. I couldn't walk out. The others did. Don called in Aidan who arrested someone. I left before I got any of the details. I just had to find you." Paul's voice dropped into prayer, his eyes closing as he did so. He sat when he finished, content for the moment. He knew that he loved Payten and wanted to spend the rest of his life with her. He thought that she loved him but he wasn't sure of that.

"Paul? Something else is going on." Payten raised her face to study the man holding her.

"There is. Don is thinking of changing how we work. He wants to change to day assignments only here in the area and to do training as we need to. He's been speaking with Abe and Richard, who changed their teams to training. We could complement each other quite well."

Payten sighed. This is what she had been praying for.

"That's been my prayer, Paul, that you don't go away for days on end. I miss you when you're gone." Her voice had dropped to the point that Paul had difficulty hearing her.

He tilted his head to watch her. He nodded. She was ready to hear what he had to say.

"Payten, we have not known each other that long. What we've been going through has brought us closer. We've talked a lot about ourselves and our lives and our dreams. We share a strong faith. Would you be my lady for life? I love you." Paul bit at his lip, not sure if he had run ahead of God in telling her that. He didn't think that he had but he was so uncertain as to the timing in telling her.

Payten stared at him before her face softened. He had said what she had dreamed that he would say.

"I will, Paul. I will. I love you too. I just thought that it was too soon to have those feelings." Payten accepted his kiss before her head was on his shoulder. "We're in danger, Paul."

"I know. I hate that this is affecting you the way it is." Paul sat in silence for a moment, not quite sure what to say. "We could marry, Payten, but that's not fair to you. You deserve to be courted, taken out for dinners, go for walks, receive flowers, and just what it is that courting couples do."

Payten nodded, knowing that Paul would have thought this through and prayed it through before he spoke.

"But what if this is all we have? This short time? Do we want to spend it apart, Paul, or together?" Payten prayed as she spoke. She knew what she wanted and where she felt God was leading them, but she would wait for Paul. He would be the spiritual head of their family, if a family is what they became.

"I get what you're saying, Payten. I just don't want to rush you." Paul's hold tightened on her, his prayer for them whispering in her ears.

"Paul? Look at it like this. God brought us together. He'll protect us." Payten looked around as she heard the back door open and close. "And here is Daci." She grinned at her friend.

Daci grinned back before she looked at Paul.

"Paul? What did you go and do?"

"Me? Nothing." His eyes narrowed as he stared at her. "Just what do you mean?"

"I mean that Don called, asking if you were here. He doesn't do that unless something happened." Daci waited patiently for her friend to speak.

Paul sighed. His eyes were on Payten who was looking between himself and Daci.

"Someone was waiting outside of the building today. Aidan arrested him. And I have no details on who or why." Paul was frustrated, to say the least.

"That's what Don said." Daci slumped into a chair for a moment before she straightened up. "You two need to do something fun. Tomorrow is an off day for us all. How be we find something fun to do?" Her grin was infectious.

"I like that idea, Daci. I've been reading through how God protects and defends us. He doesn't want us to have a spirit of fear or fright. We need to take precautions but we still have to live." Payten turned her face towards Paul, finding him nodding at her words.

"It's true, Payten sweetheart. That's what He does. We do need to take precautions but we still have to live."

Payten was nodding, her eyes on Daci. Daci was grinning at her.

"Daci? You're up to something. I can tell."

Daci began to laugh, knowing that Payten had read her correctly.

"We need to go to the zoo. I haven't been there in ages." Daci continued to laugh as Payten was staring at her before she was nodding. Paul simply stared between the two ladies and then up at Don as he appeared. "Don? Did you hear what your sister has decided we need to do?"

"I did. And I agree. We need to do something fun for a day. You need to set aside what you're going through." Don's hand was up as Payten's mouth opened to protest. "We'll take precautions as a matter of course but we do need to do this for you. Now, early morning, Daci?"

"Of course. We'll be in line as soon as they open. Now, we need to spend some time in prayer. I know from Payten that they're not receiving all the letters, threats, and packages that normally come through. That tells me that someone is very close to you two." Daci turned to Don. "And that's what you've discovered."

"It is. We'll set it aside for tonight and then play tomorrow. We haven't done that in a long time, Daci. Thank you. Life has gotten in our way and taken our spirits down to some extent."

Chapter 33

The next morning found the four standing in line for the zoo. Paul and Don had talked before they left, knowing that this was putting Paul and Payten out into the open. Were they ready for that, Paul had been asked. He had simply shrugged, knowing that they were always at risk and would be until the people responsible were arrested.

Payten leaned against Paul for a moment, her hand tight in his. She felt free that morning, free from danger and hurting. Paul had done that for her. She was grateful for that. Payten also knew that God was working in her life, letting her find the freedom that she needed so badly.

Paul exchanged a glance with Don, nodding at the question on his face. They were being followed. Both men had had glimpses of three men in the back of the line whose attention was on the quartet rather than the attractions.

"How do we do this, Don? The ladies want to have fun. They deserve to have that." Paul watched Payten as she laughed with Daci. Both ladies seemed more lighthearted that morning. "I want to give them a good day. Only, I'm not sure that we can."

"We'll do our best, Paul. It's what we always do. Come on. Let's get you to your lady." Don walked forward to stand beside his sister, an amused look on his face as they laughed at him. "What's the joke?"

The ladies looked at each other and then shrugged. They were glad to be out and about, as it's said, but they were still concerned. They were determined to set aside their fears and party, as Daci said. They both were aware of the danger but knew and trusted that God would protect them.

Three hours later with their faces flushed with happiness and laughter, Payten and Daci headed to find a table for their meal. The two men had walked the opposite way to find something for them to eat. Payten hugged Daci before she sat, laughter bubbling up inside her. She didn't think that she had had so much fun, ever, in her life.

"I'm glad that you agreed to come, Payten. We both needed this. We deal with some horrible stuff on the job." Daci sat on the opposite side of the picnic table. She dropped her head for a moment, a prayer of thanks raising from her as well as a prayer for her friend.

"We do. So do the guys. I don't know that Paul has been this lighthearted since we met. He has a wicked sense of humour." Payten grinned as Daci began to laugh even harder.

"He does. He hides it well, but it's there. You're bringing out the lightness that he has been hiding."

"I'm glad. He's good for me. Just don't tell him that." Payten's face was alight with mischief as she felt an arm across her shoulder.

"Don't tell who what?" Paul was laughing at her as he sat beside her.

"We're not telling." Payten shoved at him before she leaned against him. The love that they had for one another was obvious to the brother and sister sitting across from them.

Daci and Don shared a look before Don shrugged. He was seeing the Paul from a number of years ago, before life got busy and hectic and wore them down. He felt in his heart that the way that he wanted to take the team was the right move. It was something that he had felt that God had been leading him towards now for years.

Their meal finished, Don gathered up their garbage, heading for the trash receptacles. He could hear the laughter as the other three moved away, heading for the butterfly building. Don smiled once more. *Daci was right, once more, wasn't she, Lord? We really needed this, a chance to just walk away from our problems and study the world that You created before You created man.*

A few moments later, Don heard screams and spun, running towards where he knew that the trio had headed. He slid to a halt before he shouldered his way through the crowd. He stopped before he was on his knees, a hand reaching to rest on Paul's chest. Paul lay sprawled on his back, blood oozing from a wound in his chest. Don drew a deep breath. Paul was alive but he didn't know exactly how hurt that he was.

On his feet as the paramedics approached, Don searched for Daci and Payten. He could not see them in the crowd. He began to fear for them. Searching through the crowd, he didn't see them, approaching an officer who stood nearby.

———

"My sister, Daci, and Paul's girlfriend, Payten, are missing." Don rubbed at his head, fear beginning to raise its head inside of him.

"Don? They're missing? How long?" The officer knew Don well.

"Maybe fifteen minutes. Paul and the ladies had headed for here as I dumped the trash from our meal. I heard screams and ran here. They weren't even gone from me for five minutes. I found Paul like that." Don pointed at his friend, watching carefully as the paramedics headed off with the stretcher holding Paul. "I ran here, found him, but not the ladies. Where are they?"

"We'll look for them. How were they dressed, Don?" The officer watched as Don sent him a text with a photo from that day. "Payten has been in danger, hasn't she? I know her well from work."

"She has been. She's taken time off just to protect her fellow employees. We came here today for a day to relax and have some fun. Now, they're gone." Don was growing increasingly worried about the two as well as worrying about Paul.

Aidan appeared at last, a hand on Don's arm drawing him away from the scene.

"Talk to me, Don. I know that you've given your statement. Here, let me have your keys. We have Paul's. Someone will drive them to your homes. You're coming with me. We're heading to find Paul." Aidan's hand on Don's arm propelled the other man to Aidan's car where he shoved him inside. Once behind the wheel, Aidan took off, driving as fast as was safe.

"Aidan?" Don shook his head, coming back to the present and realizing that he was now in a vehicle.

"We're heading for the hospital. I have someone with Paul. The officers are searching for Payten and Daci. They'll keep me updated." Aidan didn't say that he had put out a call to Don's team, who were shocked at the news and promised to meet the two at the hospital.

"Thanks, Aidan. This is taking so much from everyone. Toryn is worried about Payten and her team. It almost seems as if this is being done to fracture the team or discredit Payten."

Aidan stared at Don for a few seconds before his eyes went back to the road.

"What did you just say?" Aidan's voice lashed at Don.

"What? What I said? That someone is trying to discredit Payten and through her the team? That's the conclusion that I've come to. I haven't had a chance to speak with her or my team. God brought that to my attention early this morning. I didn't want to ask her and spoil the day that we had planned. It was a day that was so badly needed by all of us."

"It was. Now, this has happened. I'll talk to the officers who are getting statements. Once I can get a clear picture of what happened and have a chance to hopefully speak with Paul, then I'll speak with Toryn. With your statement, I think that was where our investigation was heading. We have nothing on Payten other than her work. And that is concerning. We don't want to have cases thrown out of court because someone tampered with the evidence.”

“And that’s what they’re trying to do, isn’t it? So, how do we stop them, Aidan? And how do we find them?” Don waited as Aidan parked before the two men began to pray. Leaving the car, they walked rapidly into the Emergency Department, looking for the charge nurse who directed them to the room where Paul was being evaluated.

Chapter 34

Watching the physician from where he stood in the corner of the room, Don prayed for his friend. He knew that God was in control and that God was the Great Physician. He also acknowledged that Paul was in God's hands and that what was in God's will would happen. Don worried about his sister and Payten. He didn't like that the ladies had disappeared without any trace that he knew about.

Aidan had approached the physician, who had turned slightly to speak with him. Aidan stepped back, rubbing at his forehead. The word on Paul was not what he wanted to hear. The bullet had hit Paul from close range and had nicked a lung. It was now lodged in his chest. Paul was heading for surgery to remove it.

"Don?" Aidan's voice roused Don from his prayers. "The physician wants to speak with you. We'll wait in an adjacent room. I've okayed it." Aidan pointed to the doorway. "And I have an update on the search for Daci and Payten."

Don slumped in a chair, his face buried in his hands. His friend was facing surgery. He had signed the consent for that as Paul's next of kin. His sister and another friend were missing. He felt empty and lost, unable to think coherently for a moment.

Feeling a hand on his shoulder, Don looked up to see his team surrounding him. On his feet, he studied each one.

"Okay, fellows. This is where we need to start our own search. Paul's heading for surgery shortly." Don nodded at the soft comments from his team. "Now, we need to start looking for the ladies."

"What do you know, Don?" Mark asked the question for the other three.

"Not a lot. They had moved away from me towards the butterfly building. I was getting rid of our trash. It was only a couple of moments when I heard the scream. The ladies were gone by the time I reached Paul." Don nodded towards Aidan who stood just inside the closed door. "Aidan has been trying to find out what he can for us. Aidan? What can you tell us?"

"There were three men involved, Don. Two took the ladies away. When Paul tried to intervene, he was shot. From what the witnesses have said, the weapon had a silencer on it. Thankfully, no other onlookers were threatened. We have descriptions of the three men or as much of a description as we can get. We have determined that they were wearing disguises."

"That's par for the course." Caleb nodded, his thoughts going to Paul. "What can we do, Aidan?"

"For now? Stay with Don and Paul. They both will likely become targets or more of a target than they already are. With you four taking that up, it will free our men and women to search for the two ladies." Aidan walked away, the door closing behind him. He found Toryn waiting for him.

"Aidan? How's Paul?" Toryn was worried about his friend as well as the two ladies.

"Heading for surgery. They're not sure what all has been damaged until they get in there." Aidan pointed towards the exit. "Can we walk while we talk, Toryn?"

"We can, Aidan. I know that you were on scene. Give me your impressions." Toryn waited patiently for Aidan to sort through his thoughts.

"I can do that, Toryn. It was very bold and brazen of the men to kidnap the two ladies in plain sight and around people. We have tracked them to the service road behind the butterfly building. Our feeling is that they were followed all day until the ladies were with just one of the men. Don did mention that the ladies were separated from them for a few minutes while they got the food but they were in plain sight of the men. That precluded any kidnapping at that point. The onlookers really have not helped. They were more concentrated on their own families, which is what you would expect. An older fellow did give a good description of the three men but his impression was that they were disguised."

"That is what I understood." Toryn paused walking for a moment, his thoughts troubled. "With Payten? What are your thoughts?"

"Don had an interesting comment. He stated that maybe it was to go after Payten's work and discredit her." Aidan waited patiently for Toryn to mull over what he had stated.

"I think that Don's right about that. It has never seemed right another way. And with Paul? I think someone is after Don. Somehow, the two parties are connected."

"Those are my thoughts too, Toryn. I'm just not getting the connection between them." Aidan was puzzled by that.

"None of us are at the moment. It will come." Toryn turned to face the hospital. "I need to run, Aidan. I have that meeting to get to. Keep me updated." He walked away, leaving Aidan staring at the ground.

Aidan looked up to find Don and the other four men standing in front of him, grim looks on their faces. He sighed to himself. This is where it became dangerous for the two ladies. They needed to find them and find them fast.

"Aidan? What do you know?" Mark spoke up.

"Not a lot, Mark. How's Paul? Is he in surgery yet?" Aidan studied the five men, seeing the stress on their faces.

"He's just gone up. They're not sure how long it will take. Where can we meet for now?" Thomas pointed back towards the hospital. "There's a room on the surgical floor that they've cleared for us to use." He walked back towards the hospital, the other men following.

Aidan hesitated for a moment, his eyes on the sky. It was coming up to late afternoon. That worried him. He needed to find the ladies, but with no information on who had taken them, that was almost impossible.

———

Don waited for Aidan near the door, his eyes compassionate as he studied his friend. This was difficult for him, Don knew. He had seen it with the other detectives who had worked the adventures that their friends had had.

"Don? What can I do for you?" Aidan paused beside Don, seeing Gideon walking their way. He had reached out to the pastor, who had promised to be there as soon as he was able to.

"I'm not sure, Aidan. Gideon? I thought that you would show up at some point. Thank you." Don drew in a deep breath. "I just want my sister back. And Paul needs Payten here with him. How do we do that?"

Chapter 35

Paul moved restlessly, his head tossing as he strove to awake. It was a losing battle, he decided. He didn't know where he was or why he hurt the way he did. He also couldn't understand why it hurt so much to breathe. His movements stopped as he slept again, the pain medications dropping him into a drug-induced sleep.

Don watched from the bedside, Joshua on the other side. The men had refused to leave. The other three were in the waiting room. None were planning on going home. They would sleep there. It would not be the first time that they had.

"Don? How bad was it?" Joshua looked over at his team leader.

"Bad enough. There was lung damage, which we knew about. The bleeding has been stopped. They put in a chest tube for drainage of the lung. Once they can remove it, they will. He's in for a period of recovery." Don bit at his lip. Paul's injury would change the dynamics of how they worked.

"Caleb has brought in a list of what we have upcoming. Abe and Richard both reached out to see what they could do to help. I hear Emma is involved and will be forwarding what she finds to us and to Aidan."

"That's good news." Don studied the equipment surrounding Paul. He was frustrated at having Paul there. It should not have happened. "I should have been there, Joshua. I was only a minute or two behind them."

"They were watched that closely. Paul would have tried to stop them. Did no one else help?" Joshua was puzzled at that.

"They didn't have time, I suspect. And with Paul being shot, that would have stopped anyone from trying to move in and help. I can't fault them for that." Don was desperate to know where Daci was. All he could do was pray that God would protect the two ladies.

"Don? This is going to affect our work. We'll need to go over what we have on the books." Thomas had appeared, worried about Paul. It was late at night, the end of a long worrying day.

"It will." Don rubbed at his cheek. "We'll go over it tomorrow. I'll slip home and grab the contracts." He looked up as Thomas held up a folder. "Ahead of me there, Thomas, once more. Thank you. I know none of us will leave. As far as the hospital is concerned, we're security for Paul. He needs it. Joshua, you're in the room first. Two hour shifts each." Don took the folder handed to him and walked away.

"He's hurting in a way that I've never seen." Thomas watched him close the door behind him.

"He is. He wants Daci home. It's his sister that is affected. I wish that I knew where they were. I'd go in and bring both of them back."

———

"All of us would." Thomas simply bowed his head, petitioning God for healing for their friends and the return of the two ladies. He was just afraid that they would not be alive when they came home.

Don's head went back on the wall behind him. He was desperately praying for his sister and for Payten. If he knew where they were, he would have walked in and rescued them, not even considering his own safety. He also prayed for Paul. Don still didn't understand how the men had been able to ambush the trio. He prayed that Paul would be able to tell them.

Early the next morning, Paul's head began to toss and turn again. His eyes opened as he stared around. They slid closed again as he realized that he was in a hospital room. His hand felt for his chest as he prodded at it, wincing with pain.

A sound to the side of the bed had Paul turning that way, a frown on his face.

"Mark?" Paul had to swallow hard to get his words out. His throat was dry. He sipped from the straw as Mark held up a tumbler of water for him to drink from. "What happened?"

"You don't remember?" Mark set the tumbler back on the small table. "You were shot yesterday, Paul."

"I was? I don't remember." Paul moved restlessly. "Where?"

"Your chest. The bullet damaged the lung. You've had surgery to repair it. The chest tube comes out in a couple of days." Mark turned as he heard the door open. "And here is Aidan. He's been in and out a few times this morning." Mark walked towards Aidan. "Paul just woke up. He says that he can't remember anything."

Aidan shrugged, already having come to that conclusion.

"That's okay. I'll take what he gives me and work from there." Aidan walked towards Paul, finding him watching him. "Paul? I won't ask how you are since you've just awakened."

"Thanks, Aidan. I have no idea what happened. I don't remember yesterday at all if that's when it happened." He looked past him. "You're here about this. But where is Payten?"

Aidan drew in a deep breath. He would have to break the news to Paul that both Payten and Daci were still missing. That was not something that he was looking forward to having to do.

"Tell me what you can remember, Paul. I need to get what statement from you that I can." Aidan had his laptop out, ready to record Paul's statement.

"Okay. This is what I remember. Nothing. I don't remember yesterday at all. The last that I can remember is us making plans two days ago to go to the zoo. I don't remember going there at all." Paul's head went back as his eyes slid closed against the pain. "Is that sufficient?"

"It has to be. We'll readdress it as we need to. You need to inform me of what you do and don't remember as time goes on." Aidan printed off the short statement that Paul had been able to give and had him sign it. "Now, how are you feeling?"

"In a lot of pain. And it is hard to breathe." Paul rubbed at his chest again before he stared at the intravenous line running to the back of his hand. "Where's Payten?" When Aidan didn't answer right away, Paul looked up at him. "Aidan?"

"She's missing, Paul. She and Daci went missing at the time that you were shot. Witnesses said that you tried to intervene to prevent that from happening and that's when you were injured." Aidan watched with compassion as Paul's eyes slid closed and a single tear tracked down Paul's cheek.

Chapter 36

Don walked slowly back into the hospital. He had just met with Toryn and Gideon for prayer for the situation and the people involved. There had been no word yet as to where the two ladies were. As time passed, Don grew more fearful for his sister and their friend. He was also very worried about Paul. Mark had called just to let him know that Paul could not remember the day before. That was not what Don had wanted to hear. He had shared a look with Toryn as he told him what Mark had relayed.

Gideon had simply prayed for his friend, bringing in all the promises of God's defense of the ladies and Paul. Don had been grateful and thankful for that.

Thomas was waiting for him, pointing to the coffee shop. Don followed him, a frown on his face. Thomas must have some news, Don decided, to sidetrack him to the coffee shop.

"Don? Any word?" Thomas set his coffee cup down on the table before he sat, his eyes on Don.

Don shook his head. He was discouraged, he had to admit to himself, and deeply worried. It was just Daci and himself left of their family.

"How's Paul?"

"He can't remember yesterday at all. Aidan spoke with him earlier but was aware that this might have been the case. I spoke with Paul's physician. He said that Paul has likely shut down what happened, realizing that he couldn't have saved Daci and Payten." Thomas was worried about Paul.

"It is likely the case. I spent some time with Toryn and Gideon just now. The church is praying for our friends. I asked him about there being two different parties involved. Toryn agreed that it was a distinct possibility."

"That's what we think. How do we figure that out?" Thomas' eyes rose as Joshua and Caleb joined them. "Mark's with Paul?"

"He is. Paul's sleeping again. His physician was in and said that is to be expected right now and for the next couple of days." Joshua was frustrated at the turn of events.

"That he will. We need to meet again as a team, fellows." Don twisted his coffee cup in his hands, not sure where they were headed. "We need to find the ladies, fellows. How do we do that?"

"I've reached out to our sources on the street. They'll be looking for the ladies. There is also word that a hit was put out on Paul. The person who passed that one wasn't sure why and if it related to Payten or not." Caleb shared a look with Thomas. "And that's frustrating."

"It is all frustrating. Let's spend some time in prayer, fellows. All those verses that we have memorized and claimed over the years about God's defense of us and His protection are certainly needing to be claimed at this point."

———

Don walked towards Paul's hospital room, finding the physician waiting for him.

"Doc? Is he worse?" Don paused beside the physician, who stood near the nursing station.

"No, he's not. In fact, he's ahead of where I expected him to be at this point. I know that he heals well but your prayers are working in this." Bob Rogers, the physician, was a member of their church. "If he continues as he is, we'll be able to remove the chest tube in a couple of days. It's the restlessness that he's under. Where is his lady?"

"That we don't know. Paul was shot trying to protect both Payten and Daci." Don caught the quick glance that was shot his way. "We've been trying to keep that quiet. The ladies have disappeared to some place where we don't know where they are. And we don't know by whom."

Bob nodded, knowing that this was the case. Don had always been honest with him.

"Thank you for sharing that, Don. Go on in. Mark is there with him." Bob watched as Don nodded before he headed to find Paul.

Standing near Paul's bed, Don grew thoughtful. *This was bizarre,* he thought. *How did they manage to shoot Paul so quickly and then disappear with Daci and Payten? They had to be monitoring us and following us that closely.*

"Mark? Did Aidan say where the vehicle was that took Daci and Payten away?" Don waited patiently for Mark to answer.

"That's the strange thing, Don. They didn't see any evidence of a vehicle. Daci and Payten disappeared around the building on the security system and then just aren't seen again. There was no vehicle there that Aidan or his team could find."

"There wasn't? Does that mean that they're still on site?" Don spun at Mark's words.

"That's what Aidan is working on. We think that they sheltered them somewhere until the commotion died down and then walked out with them. If they forced Daci and Payten to change their appearance at all, then they could have walked out the main entrance with them and no one would have been the wiser."

Don stared at him, knowing that Mark had likely pegged exactly what had happened.

"Did you talk to Aidan?" Don thought that he would have. That was what Mark did.

"I did. He stared at me and then ran from the room. I don't know if that was looked at yesterday in more than a perfunctory manner."

"They likely searched the buildings. But where would they hold them? That's the question."

Paul had roused as they had spoken, listening to the conversation.

"There are hidden rooms in the butterfly building. We used to explore them as kids, doing our best not to get caught. I don't know if you were ever aware of that fact." Paul's voice was low and pain-filled.

"No, I don't know that I did." Don walked away, his phone out to call Aidan. "Aidan? Did you know there are hidden rooms in the butterfly building?"

Aidan started at his phone. That was a fact that no one had bothered to tell them.

"No, I didn't. Did you?" Aidan was on the move, heading for his car and then the zoo.

"Not until Paul just mentioned it. He used to explore them, he stated." Don was on the move as well. "I'm meeting you there."

Chapter 37

Aidan stared in disbelief at the older worker who was nodding. He had not been around yesterday, Aidan knew for a fact.

"You're confirming what we've been told? That there are hidden rooms in that building?"

"There are." The worker pointed towards the back of the building. "Around here. Not a lot of people are aware of them. Now, that young Paul? He spent a lot of time here when he was a teen. I know that he knew about them. We spent many hours exploring them together. He was curious as to why they were there and what their use would have been." John stopped at the back of the building, pointing to a section. "It's right here. There's a latch that opens the wall." He pushed the latch, leaving Aidan staring at the moving wall in surprise and shock.

Don stood back, knowing that he could not enter even as much as he wanted to. He had to stand back. He watched as Aidan disappeared after John, the large torch that John was holding lighting the rooms that they came upon.

Aidan's hand reached to stop John.

"We need to stop here, John. And I need you to leave. There's evidence here that we need to retrieve." Aidan followed John back outside, his phone out to call for the techs and then to call Toryn.

Toryn paced across the grass to stand beside Don. He had not thought about the hidden rooms and had been surprised when Aidan had called, simply stating that there was evidence in them that they needed to collect. He had finished what he had needed to and then approached Don.

"Don? Did you know about the rooms?"

Don hook his head.

"No, I never did. Paul mentioned them and that's why we ended up here." Don watched closely as the teams moved around both inside and outside of the building. "It makes sense, though. Grab the ladies, tuck them in here, changed their appearance, and then just walk out with them at closing time. Mingle with the crowd and who would notice them?" Don was furious that this may have happened.

Toryn nodded before he grabbed at Don's arm.

"Come on. Let's head for the security office. Maybe we can catch a glimpse of them leaving." Toryn simply made his request, and the security officer pulled up the video stream for them.

Don and Toryn concentrated closely on the video before Don asked to have it stopped. His finger pointed at two couples.

"That's them, Toryn. They just walked out with them. Daci and Payten are not fighting them."

"No. They wouldn't. The people around them would have been threatened as would have you and the rest of your team. That you would not have known. Your thoughts were that they were taken away right away." Toryn asked for a copy of the video feed, which the security officer gladly provided. He tucked the thumb drive into an evidence bag and walked away from the office, Don beside him.

"Toryn?" Aidan turned as he heard Toryn call his name. "We found evidence that they were kept there for a while. Nothing to say where they are now."

"They changed the ladies' appearance and walked them right out of the front entrance in the exiting crowd." Toryn handed over the bag with the thumb drive. "Here's that evidence."

Aidan looked at the bag and then at Toryn. He nodded. Toryn had found what they needed. Now, they just needed to find the ladies.

Paul looked up a short time later as Don and Toryn approached his bed. He was hurting physically but the emotional hurt felt much worse. He knew that Payten and Daci were in God's hands but that didn't make it any easier to bear.

"Paul? How are you?" Toryn watched him closely, seeing that he was in pain.

"Not great. I want out of here to search for Payten and Daci." Paul's head went back on the pillow as his eyes slid closed.

"No, I didn't expect that you would be feeling totally like yourself. Have you remembered anything more?" Toryn's gaze rose to Mark and then to Don, who was nodding.

"No, I haven't. I wish that I could." Paul's eyes opened as he frowned at Toryn. "You have news." His words were a statement and not a question.

"We do. You were correct about the hidden rooms in the building. The ladies were held there until the zoo closed. We have footage that shows their appearances were altered."

Paul nodded, knowing where this was going.

"They walked them out with the crowd. Not one of us would have expected that. I thought that they would have had a vehicle on the service road behind the building." Paul shared a look with Don and saw the worry and fear that he was trying hard to hide. "Don? What do we do now?"

"For now? We let Aidan and his team work it. We will as well, Paul. You can't. Not for now. Your task is to heal." Don walked away, leaving Mark with Paul.

Aidan turned from the photocopier as he heard Toryn's voice. He gathered up his papers and walked towards the police chief and the head of the lab.

"Toryn? You wanted something?"

"I do. I need you to work with Peter on this." Toryn held up the bag with the flash drive. "This is the evidence that we recovered from the zoo."

Aidan reached for the bag and nodded. This might help find the ladies but he was confident that it would. Peter pointed towards Aidan's office before the two men walked that way.

"Peter? Toryn spoke with you?"

"He did." Peter sank into a chair, frustrated and disheartened for a moment. "I hate this, Aidan. Someone is after Payten and I want that person. We have gone back over the cases that she has worked on. So far, we don't feel that any were compromised. Toryn called in another force to investigate."

"That he would do. I am told that so far it's been safe with no compromise of the evidence. The cases that she's been working on since this started?" Aidan was hesitant to state what he thought.

"We're focusing on those, especially since we found the equipment that had been hidden." Peter pointed to the evidence bag that was still in Aidan's hand. "Let's take a look at that, Aidan. I want to keep it just between us three until we need to put it out. That will be later today."

Chapter 38

Three days later, Paul nodded at Thomas as he helped him into the house. Thomas had volunteered to stay with him, given his paramedic training. The physician had not wanted him to leave the hospital yet but had simply nodded as Paul had stared him down.

Sinking into his bed, Paul groaned. He was not sure that he had made the right move but he could not stay there and not search for his lady. And he couldn't do that at the hospital.

Thomas removed Paul's sneakers and then helped him to settle down before he pulled the covers over him. He watched his friend closely before he walked quietly away and to the kitchen. The other four team members were there.

"Is Paul asleep?" Caleb's voice broke into the silence of the room.

"He is. He should not have come home." Thomas was frustrated with that fact and the fact that Paul had been hurt. "Where do we go from here, Don?"

"We don't have a lot of information. I spoke with Emma this morning. She was horrified to hear of what has happened. She's been out of the area until now but will make this a priority now. I got the impression that she had an idea of who it might be when I explained what all had happened and where."

Don reached to pour their coffee before pointing to Paul's office. "We'll meet in there."

The men made no progress on their investigation. That puzzled them. They should have been able to, they all knew. They rose at last, all leaving but Thomas.

Don stood in his living room, his eyes on the front door. He was uneasy for some reason. He had learned to trust those instincts. Instead of heading for bed, Don sought the chair that he used as his prayer corner and spent the night in prayer, having to come to the conclusion that God was in ultimate control. It was up to God how the ladies came home. Don had to be prepared that it may not be in the way that they all prayed for.

That morning, Paul rose. While not steady on his feet and still in pain somewhat, he felt somewhat better. Thomas turned as he approached the kitchen, a frown on his face that cleared as he studied Paul.

"Paul? Feeling better?" Thomas grinned at him for a moment.

"I do. Let's eat before we spend some time in prayer. I just have the sense that today is crucial in the ladies coming home." Paul didn't see Thomas nod. Paul was known for having had these feelings before which had saved their lives on occasion.

"We can do that. Now, what do you feel like?" Thomas reached for the pot to do scrambled eggs and dropped bread into the toaster. He didn't feel like eating and he didn't think that Paul did either.

Paul's head raised during their time of prayer. A sound had come to his ear. He listened carefully before he shook his head and then bowed it once more. He didn't know that the answer to their prayers was standing on the porch.

Paul rose when the two men had finished their prayer time, stretching as best as he could. A frown covered his face before he shrugged and headed back for the kitchen. A sound on the front porch had the two men staring at one another. As far as they knew, their team was not to be there until later that day due to work constraints. And Aidan hadn't said that he would be around that day.

Paul pulled the door open and just stood, his mouth dropping open. He barely had time to brace himself, Thomas' hand flat on his back to provide support, before a lady was in his arms, her own arms locked around his neck. The pain in his chest hit for a moment and staggered him.

Thomas looked past him, his eyes on Daci before he moved Paul and Payten out of the way and was reaching for Daci. Daci almost ran into the house before Thomas had slammed the door behind him and was searching outside. His phone was out to call Aidan and then Don, having to leave a voice mail message just stating that Don needed to call him as soon as he could.

Aidan walked into Paul's living room, his eyes on the ladies. Daci simply shook her head, knowing that he was questioning what all that they may have said.

"We haven't said anything, Aidan, except ask for clean clothes. Thomas took me to Don's to grab some. We felt so filthy and unkempt."

Payten was silent, her eyes on Aidan. She made no effort to move from where she sheltered in Paul's arms. Aidan could see the pain on Paul's face but also knew that there was no way that he would ever let go of Payten. And he needed him to do just that.

"I need to get your statements, ladies. Daci, you're first. We'll just use Paul's office." Aidan stalked off that way, knowing that Paul would not hesitate to let him use it.

Daci followed him, her statement given quickly. She turned for a moment before she spoke.

"Paul? How is he?"

"He had lung damage from when he was shot. He'll be a while healing but the physician thinks that he'll heal fully." Aidan waited patiently for Payten to appear, standing in the hallway watching for her. He could hear her voice for a moment before she appeared, stopping for a moment just out of sight of the living room. Aidan knew that she was watching Paul, noting the changes in him that had been caused by her, or that was how he assumed that she was thinking.

"Payten?" Aidan's voice was quiet and gentle. Nevertheless, Payten jumped at the sound.

Payten walked slowly towards Aidan, knowing that she had to speak with him and give her statement. She wasn't sure if she was ready to do that but she had to. That had to be done before many more minutes passed.

"Aidan?" Payten's voice was subdued, not at all her usual tone.

Aidan nodded to himself. This had taken a toll on both ladies but particularly Payten. He would need to find someone for her to speak with. He nodded again. He knew just the lady

"Payten? You do need to talk with me. It's not an option." He watched with compassion on his face as she struggled with her emotions. "Take your time, Payten. Paul's not going anywhere."

"But he was hurt because of me. How do I live with that?" Payten swiped at her face, taking with thanks the handkerchief that was handed to her.

"With God's help, Payten. Paul loves you enough that he put himself in the way of danger for you. He would have done that for anyone."

Chapter 39

Aidan waited patiently for Payten to gather her thoughts and speak. He sighed to himself. Something else had happened, that much he knew. Would Payten tell him? He wasn't sure about that, not any more. Payten may well hide it from him. He begged God to open Payten up again and let her speak what she needed to, no matter how much it hurt.

Payten shuddered as she thought back over the past few days. She had been terrified, she had to admit to herself. Just how did she explain it to Aidan, she wasn't quite sure.

"Payten?" Aidan's voice had her looking up at him. "Just start talking. I'll record it. Then we'll go over it."

"Okay. It's hard, Aidan. They threatened the men. They threatened you. I don't get why though. It's not clear." Payten reached for the bottle of water that Aidan handed her, opening it to take a sip before twisting the cap back onto it.

"Just talk, Payten. We'll sort it out afterwards, what you tell us." Aidan was prepared for that. He could hear soft conversation in the living room, knowing that Paul was anxious to be back with Payten. That wasn't happening anytime soon. He prayed harder for his friend.

"Okay. I guess that I can do that." Payten still hesitated to speak, the words that had been lashed at her in anger causing her fear of speaking.

Payten's thoughts went back once more to that morning at the zoo. She felt once more the happiness of that morning. Paul had teased her about many things yet kept her hand tight in his. She had seen a different side to him that day.

Once their lunch had finished, they had decided to head for the butterfly building. Butterflies had always fascinated Payten from her early memories. She had been almost dancing as they walked that way. There had been a number of people around but she hadn't cared. Today was about having fun and relaxing. They had all agreed that was needed.

Her steps slowed as they approached the building. She frowned at the three men waiting in front of them. Her head shook as she realized that she didn't know them but she didn't think that they were there for anyone's good.

"You two ladies are coming with us." The shorter of the men spoke, his voice obviously disguised.

Paul moved to stand in front of the women, a hand shoving Payten and then Daci behind him.

"I don't think so." Paul prayed that Don would arrive in the next few seconds. He wasn't sure that he could protect the ladies if anything happened. The odds of three to one were not great.

The men moved closer to them, two flanking the trio. Paul's eyes were in constant motion, trying to watch all three. That was an impossibility.

"They're coming with us." The man in front of him raised a weapon, discharging it.

Paul's body flew backwards to land on the ground. He sprawled awkwardly, blood starting to cover his chest. Payten screamed and scrambled to reach him. An arm around her waist trapped her arms to her side. She struggled to escape, lifted up into the arm. Her feet kicked at the man holding her to no avail.

Daci was similarly treated. Her arms trapped to her side as well, she too was picked up and carried away. The two ladies heard the screams behind them and the shouts of the men. The families scattered quickly, the fathers standing by. One man was on his knees beside Paul even as Don approached.

The men carrying the ladies disappeared behind the building. The first man reached for a certain portion of the wall, pulling it open and then closed after they had entered. The men strode rapidly towards a room, dropping the ladies to their feet but keeping a hand on their arms. The first man shut the door and locked it behind him, standing outside of the room, listening for anyone coming after them. He realized that they were in the clear for now. He nodded. This had not gone quite as they had planned but the ladies were in their custody and that was what they had been ordered to do.

Set on their feet, Payten and Daci looked at one another and then ran for the door. Payten tugged at it to open it even as she felt her arm grabbed once more. She was pulled back from the door. She drew in a sobbing breath as she felt cold steel click around her wrists. She had been handcuffed. Shoved to the floor in a corner of the room, Payten watched in horror as Daci received the same treatment and was then shoved to another corner of the room.

Hours passed as the men waited patiently. This was not the first time that they had been through this. Closing time at the zoo found the ladies pulled to their feet. Capes were thrown around their shoulders and hats shoved down on their heads. Led from the room, the ladies were shoved outside of the building. The men kept a hand on their arms, ordering them to keep their faces down. They were forced to walk to the exit and through it. Walked forward to the edge of the parking lot, Payten drew in a deep breath. *This is it, isn't it, Lord? We disappear and are never seen again. Only, I don't know why. I'm not sure that any of us know why. Please protect Paul and Don and their team. Help our friends to solve this soon without anyone else being hurt. I don't know how badly Paul was hurt. I can only pray that he is still alive.*

Daci watched closely, her training from her brother kicking in to observe the men and the vehicle. A van, she decided, that was used for deliveries. She couldn't see outside of it, not from where they were sitting on the floor. Her shoulder touched Payten, bringing some comfort to each of them.

Driven around for a while, the ladies were finally pulled from the van in a rough manner and then pulled into a house through a basement door. The door was locked behind them from the outside. The handcuffs were removed as were the disguises. The men walked away, leaving Payten and Daci standing in the centre of the furnished room.

Payten ran for the door, yanking at it. It just didn't budge. Daci, meanwhile, searched for a way out, checking the windows and then the door at the top of the stairs. All were locked up tight.

Daci stood once more in the centre of the room, Payten pacing in a circle around her.

"Who are these men, Daci?" Payten finally stopped, her eyes focusing on the door to the outdoors.

"I have no idea, Payten. They're not saying." Daci reached to hug her friend.

"And Paul? Is he even still alive?" Payten's sobs shook her body.

"I'm sure that he is. There were people moving towards him as we were taken away. I had forgotten about that hidden room. I'm not sure if Don ever knew about it." Daci walked the perimeter of the room once more, trying to figure out a way to escape.

"I pray that he is. This is bizarre, you know. Who is behind this?" Payten was throwing out a question without really expecting an answer.

Chapter 40

Two days passed in the same manner. There was food brought down from the upstairs for them three times a day. Payten refused to eat it, preferring just to drink water from the tap in the small bathroom that they had found. Daci had stared at the food and then agreed with Payten. She was not taking any chance that the food was tampered with.

On the third day of their captivity, the two ladies awoke in the early morning. They looked at one another before they were on their feet, shoving their shoes on. Payten headed for the outside door, pulling at it. A shocked look of surprise crossed her face as it opened. Daci shook her head, her finger on her lips to silence any comment that Payten might make.

The two ladies were out of the basement and running for the street that they could see behind them. They ran as far as they could before they stopped, dropping to the lawn and trying to catch their breath. They raised their heads at last, staring at each other in shock that they had been able to walk, no, run, from the house.

"What just happened, Daci?" Payten spoke at long last, her eyes on her friend.

"We ran from our captors. I don't understand. I thought that they had locked everything up. It was when we went to sleep last night."

"I know. I heard a sound this morning that woke me up. You woke up at the same time." Payten drew in a deep breath, ready to run again. "Where are we?"

"I heard the same noise, I think. It was a bang, likely on the door. Someone found us and freed us. We're not safe yet, though." Daci was on her feet, a hand out to help Payten up. "I know where we are, Payten. We're about twenty blocks from Paul's home."

"We're that close? How many blocks did we run?" Payten took off on a run again, this time slower, finding Daci running as well.

"About fifteen, I think. Come on. We'll head for Paul's. If no one is there, we'll go to one of his neighbours. They'll help us out. That's the kind of neighbours that he has." Daci paused as she approached Paul's home, a hand out to stop Payten. "Hold on a moment, Payten. Let's make sure that no one is around."

Payten nodded, her eyes roving over the area before she was running across the street and up the steps to the front door. Daci knocked at it, waiting for it to open. Once inside, they simply shook their heads, Payten searching for Paul. Once safe in Paul's arms, she began to relax. She didn't care what had happened or that she had to give her statement. Paul was still alive and she was here in his arms. *Thank you, Lord. I am so thankful that Paul is alive. I can tell that he is hurting but I am grateful that we are together again. Now, Lord, we need to solve this and I don't know how.*

———

Payten came back to the present, her eyes on Aidan. Aidan had been puzzled at what had happened.

"You weren't asked for anything? Not told to do something?"

"Not all. We didn't see anyone except when the meals were brought down to us. There was never anything said to us. It was just so strange. I don't understand why we were just left alone."

"That was done to wear you down. It would have happened if you had stayed there for long. Even with two of you together, you would have gone into the hole that they were waiting for you to drop into. At that point, you would have been more vulnerable to what they were going to ask you to do. And that is something that we're trying to work through." Aidan looked down at his notes, raising his head as Payten gave a small sound. "Payten? What did you just think?"

"The English case. I was working on it. That's when this all started. Has it been solved yet?" Payten's face had paled as she thought through the case.

Aidan's face grew stern. He knew exactly what she wasn't saying. Someone on the force had let slip or said deliberately that Payten was working on that case.

"No, we're not. I'm contacting your boss. We're sending that case out to another lab. They'll work on it and see if they confirm what you found. I am confident that they will."

"That is if the evidence has not already been tampered with." Payten's face grew bleak.

"It's okay, Payten. We locked up all the evidence that you had been working on from just before this started. Toryn asked for that, thinking ahead. No one has had a chance to tamper with it."

"That's a relief." Payten looked towards the door. "How is Paul? I know that he won't tell me."

"He was shot in the chest, as you know. The bullet did damage the lung. He's off work now for a while to let it heal. And heal it will. That we are confident of. We just need to resolve this." Aidan watched Payten closely, seeing her face tighten. "Payten? What did you just think about?"

Payten opened her mouth and then closed it. She was about to accuse someone and she wasn't sure of the facts.

"I think I know who is behind this." She said a name, watching as Aidan nodded. "You think the same?"

"That's the conclusion that we have been coming to. And Toryn thinks the same. The problem is to keep you and Paul safe until we have all the evidence we need."

"And you're not going to get all the evidence if we stay hidden. We haven't been getting the usual stuff that people get when they're undergoing this. That tells me that someone is close to us and watching us too closely."

———

"We agree with that, Payten." He rose, tucking away all his paperwork. "I'm off to the office. I'll speak with Toryn and then we'll make some plans. We'll do our best to keep you safe, Payten. We have officers volunteering that all the time. They were out searching for you. Now, do we need to have you two assessed by a physician?"

"We do. I would suggest Tom Olsen. He's an emergency room physician but also a member of our church. We don't have a lot of contact, I don't think. It should be okay." Payten was hesitant to suggest anyone.

"I'll call him. I know that he's not working today. We'll find some clean clothes for you two as well."

"Daci was looking after that, she said. Thank you, Aidan. You don't know how much this means to me." Payten walked away, desperate to find Paul. She just needed to be held by him and prayed for.

Chapter 41

Paul watched Payten as she slept, his arm still around her. She had not wanted to move too far from him and he had not wanted her too far from him. But he did need to rise. He nodded as Thomas approached, helping to raise Payten from his shoulder with Daci there to help him to stand. Thomas laid Payten back down on the couch, tucking a pillow under her head before Daci covered her.

Letting Thomas help him to the bedroom, Paul stood for a moment, his head hanging down. He needed to shower and shave. He just didn't know if he had the energy to do just that. Thomas simply helped him, knowing that Paul would never ask.

Feeling somewhat refreshed, Paul sat for a moment on the side of the bed. Thomas had walked away, intent on finding Don and their team mates. On his feet, he stopped beside the couch, studying Payten. He thanked God that He had spared her and Daci and returned them home.

He turned as he heard voices in the hallway. His eyes closed as he heard Don's voice, happiness and relief in it as he found Daci. The other three of his team mates were there as well, coming to find him. Their eyes searched his face before they dropped to Payten, who still slept, exhaustion showing in the dark circles under her eyes.

"Paul? How are you feeling?" Mark reached to lay a hand on Paul's shoulder, his prayer raised for his friend.

Paul shrugged, not sure how to respond.

"Where do we stand in the investigation, Mark?"

"Not where we need to be. That's a given." Mark stared around, seeing Daci near him. "Daci?"

"We were held about thirty-five blocks from here, Mark. This is the name of whose place it is. I have passed it on to Samuel as well. He's agreed to do a property search on it. And I have given it to Emma/"

"That's good. Emma will work her magic." Joshua's hand reached out to steady Paul. "Paul, you need to sit. Here. Into the kitchen. I don't expect that you've eaten much."

Paul shook his head, his eyes on Payten.

"No, I haven't. Something light sounds good."

"We have soup ready, Paul." Daci walked away, knowing that Paul would follow when he was ready.

Paul bent to kiss Payten, his hand resting on her hair. He was grateful that she was safe with him but the danger was not over. That he knew only too well.

"We need to solve this, fellows. And now." His voice was harsh with worry. "I can't do this again. Neither can Payten or Daci."

"We understand, Paul." Joshua's hand reached out to turn Paul towards the kitchen and the nourishment that he needed.

Late that evening, Paul sank gratefully into his bed. Payten still slept, exhaustion keeping her that way. Daci had settled down in one of the spare rooms, grateful to be free. Her prayers were rising. Don had claimed the couch in the office. The other four men had left but had promised to be there early in the morning.

Aidan rose from his desk at home. He had been sent from the office and told to take the night off. He just couldn't. He had driven by the home where the ladies had been held. A frown had covered his face before he nodded. Aidan was sure that Payten had named the correct people. An email from Samuel with the title details had confirmed that.

He was at a loss where to proceed. He knew that the Riverville police department had taken over the investigation into the evidence that Payten had been working on. He didn't expect any response for a couple of days and was surprised that Frankie Brennan, the lead detective on that force, had reached out not even thirty minutes earlier. He simply stated that they had found some evidence that someone had tried to tamper with both the evidence and Payten's reports. He would be there in the morning. Would Aidan be available?

Payten shifted restlessly on the couch, her eyes opening for a moment. She felt fear until she looked around in the low lighting that had been left on. She drew in a deep breath. Somehow, Daci and she must have escaped. Just how that was, she couldn't remember. Her brain was not working the way it should. Her thoughts drifted back over the last few days. An almost sob rose in her throat. There had been evidence there in the basement. She had seen it but had blocked it when she had given her statement. Reaching for her phone, Payten sent a simple text off to Aidan, who responded that he would speak to her in the morning. She needed to sleep.

Payten gave a small smile before she was on her feet, heading for food and something to drink. The bottle of water in her hand had her staring at it. No, she decided. They had not been drugged or anything like that. It was as if their captors were waiting for word on what to do with them. And to be freed like that? Who had discovered where they were and let them out?

Daci roused as she heard soft footsteps. She had not settled down into a deep sleep, just unable to do so. On her feet, she moved quietly towards the living room, finding Payten standing in the centre of the room, just staring into space.

"Payten? What's troubling you?"

"Daci? You're okay?" Payten drew a breath of relief when Daci nodded. "I don't understand any of this. Do you?"

"No, I don't." Daci left and returned with her own bottle of water. "Let's sit and talk it over. We haven't done that. You were asleep almost as soon as you gave your statement. And Paul was just not letting go of you."

"That's why I slept so soundly then. His arms around me made me feel safe." Payten sighed. "Did you see the evidence in the basement?"

Daci nodded.

"I did. And I am afraid for us, particularly you. They would have known that we saw it. They'll try and kill us now, not wanting us to say anything."

"I sent a text message to Aidan. He'll be by in the morning. And he said Frankie Brennan would be with him."

"I see. He works for Riverville, I think, as a detective. Don knows him and I have met him. They must have sent the evidence to them. They wouldn't have sent it Andrew's way, not given that Phoebe, Andrew's wife, thought for years that Toryn and she were cousins."

"They did? I didn't know that." Payten drew in a deep breath. "Where is God, Daci?"

"God? He is right here with us, Payten. He was with us in the basement. I could feel His presence around us. He protects us. He defends us. He gave us peace there. Neither of us was worried, I don't think. He covered us with His hands and sheltered us in the crevice of a rock. He calmed the storm of fear within us."

Payten had turned to her friend as Daci spoke, nodding at Daci's words.

"He did all that, didn't He? It's hard to see when you're going through things but I felt His presence. There are angels surrounding us. Nothing happens to us that He doesn't allow."

Chapter 42

Payten was up and out of the house early the next morning. Aidan had appeared and whisked her away, leaving Paul staring after them, disconcerted that his lady had disappeared once more.

Unsure as to what Aidan wanted, Payten turned to him in his car to find him shaking his head. She snapped her lips closed, knowing that he would let her speak when she was able to.

Once in his office, Aidan sat behind his desk, pointing Payten to a chair. She sat, not speaking with her eyes on him. She heard footsteps that approached and sensed someone sitting beside her. She didn't turn from her staring at Aidan.

Aidan eventually raised his head, his eyes focusing on Payten, who didn't blink as she stared back at him. Frankie Brennan had arrived and been directed to Aidan's office. Aidan had glanced up briefly and nodded at him. He had a grin on his face, watching the duel between the two.

"Frankie? You've met Payten?" Aidan's question had Payten jumping.

Payten turned towards Frankie, her eyes huge. She had not realized that he had appeared and sat beside her.

"I have. Frankie? You're here?" Payten's voice was high-pitched as she struggled to control her emotions,

———

"I am. I had to come. We have looked over the evidence that was forwarded it to us. Caleb made it a priority for our teams. So far, we can't find that anything was tampered with or damaged. We are holding onto it at our site for now. Toryn has asked for that and Caleb agrees."

"That's a relief. I was so worried about that." Payten continued to stare at him.

"It is a relief. That's not to say that someone didn't try to tamper with the evidence of the cases that you were working on. We found evidence of that in the last two cases."

"They tried?" Payten swallowed hard. "Do we know who?"

"We do, Payten. I can't tell you as yet." Frankie handed over a folder to Aidan. "Aidan, this is what we discovered. We can talk once you've gone through it. For now, it is sufficient to say that both Paul and Payten are still in extreme danger. Abe offered to hide them away."

Aidan grinned at that. He knew that Abe had a security team and would have done that.

"Has Ian offered to fly them away to safety?" Aidan began to laugh as Frankie did.

Frankie found it hard to sober up enough to explain to Payten that one of Abe's men, Ian, always offered to fly the ladies in danger to safety.

"Maybe that's what we need." Payten thought about it. "No, that won't work. They'd just come looking for us. That would just delay the inevitable."

"It would be. We've been through this, Payten. We want this over for you and we'll make it happen." Frankie stayed for a while and then walked away, leaving Payten staring at the floor in Aidan's office.

"Payten? What else can we do?" Aidan's voice was steady but didn't give away anything.

"I have no idea, Aidan. If we're through, I want to leave." Payten was on her feet, moving through the building, greeting the officers and staff. She stood outside on the sidewalk, not sure where to go. She didn't have her vehicle. A voice speaking beside her had her jumping. Mark and Caleb stood there.

"Payten? Paul was worried about you and sent us to find you." Mark's gaze lifted to the stairs into the building, nodding at Aidan.

"He was? He's still at home, waiting for you to return. Are you finished here?" Mark's hand was out to catch Payten's arm and lead her to Caleb's truck. He could feel danger nearing them. "Come on, Payten. In you go." Mark shut the door behind her before he was in the front seat.

Caleb drove off, both men watching carefully. He nodded as he saw the vehicle pull away from the curb and follow him.

"We have a tail, Mark."

Mark turned, catching the plate number and then calling it in.

"I thought that we would." Mark's eyes were on Payten, seeing the discomfort and fear that she was trying hard to hide. "Payten? What can we do for you?"

"I don't know other than to solve this. How do we do that? I know Aidan's working on it, but he has so many other cases." Payten was becoming distraught, even though she kept praying. She still felt isolated from God.

"Emma's been in touch. She said that someone from there would be heading our way today. We're planning on meeting at Paul's." Mark watched as her face crumbled for a moment.

"How's Paul? We didn't get a chance to talk this morning. Aidan just showed up and took me away." Payten stared out of the side window, not wanting to see the men's feelings that she was sure would show hatred and disgust.

"He's hurting physically but that's improving. He's hurting for you, Payten. And for himself. He wants to protect you but can't. We don't know who is after you, other than the name that you have given."

"I know. We need to research him. I just don't know how to do that."

"We'll work on it for you, Payten." Caleb spoke as he pulled to a halt at Paul's home. "We'll take what we have and see what we come up with. Emma's sending us information. That means that she's found what we need. We'll look at it, take what we find, and then find this person. I have no doubt that you are correct in your statement. We've talked about that couple. There has always been something about them. None of us have ever felt comfortable around them."

"I know." Payten bit at her lip. "I just don't like accusing them without proof. That's what we need. And I know that Aidan is doing his best to find that but he has other cases that he's working on."

Paul stood just back from the truck. He had been watching for them, having received a text from Aidan that she was on her way to him. Payten stared at him through the window, a troubled look on her face. He was hurting, she knew. She was as well. She knew he loved her just as she loved him. She just didn't know if their love was enough to get them through the next few days. Her hand froze on the door handle.

"I know why, guys. I know why." She was out of the truck, in Paul's arms, sobs wracking her body.

Chapter 43

Paul stared at Payten in shock, his hand rubbing at his chest. He was in pain, he had to admit, but his lady was in worse pain from his point of view. He heard what she had asked but wasn't sure if he had heard her correctly. His eyes raised to the other five men surrounding him, seeing Richard and his team approaching through the opening front door, and then Abe and Emma following.

"What did you just say, Payten?" Paul reached to hug her, frustrated that he could only use one arm.

"That someone wanted us to connect and then destroy both of us. They wanted us to date. That's their character. I'm not clear in my mind how they planned to accomplish that." Payten shook with the force of her emotions, her arms around Paul as tightly as she could without hurting him.

Richard paused beside Don, an eyebrow raised. This was a new thought, he decided.

"I think that she's right, Richard." Don rubbed at his face. "This has been strange. They haven't received all those parcels, threats, letters, etc. that normally comes to those in danger. That fact has puzzled us all along."

"It has." Richard watched as the two ladies on his team, Silver and Naomi, moved to Daci, pulling her aside. "But the question would be as to why."

"That it is." Abe stopped beside his friends. "Emma has found some interesting information on the pair. I know that it's a little early for a meal. How be we eat and then spend time in prayer? These two need it." He shot a look at Don. "And this is far from over for your team."

"I get that, Abe. We understand that it will go through all of us, just like it has for you both. Now, we have sandwiches and salads. Daci and Joshua were busy earlier." Don pointed towards the kitchen.

"That sounds good. Emma brought veggies and dip and fruit. It's sufficient for us."

Two hours later, Don raised his head. They had managed to all gather in Paul's office, the men finding somewhere to sit on the floor. He watched as Paul's arm tightened around Payten. Don saw the devastation on her face and sighed. This is where it always got dangerous. He prayed that nothing more would happen to the couple but also was a realist. It likely would.

"Payten?" Don waited patiently for Payten to look at him. "What did you mean? What you said earlier?"

"About us dating? I think that is true. They wanted us to date and then they would destroy us. Nothing about this has made sense, other than the bomb. That would go towards what Paul does on the team. That doesn't fit with what all happened next, other than it brought Paul and me together."

"She's right there." Abe spoke up. "You haven't been through what most of the rest of us have been through. You know Richard's team's stories. You've heard ours. I know that Frankie was around this morning. He and Deirdre had an adventure, as we term it. Paul, you know what Samuel and Aideen and all their friend went through, including Bill and Andrew. This is where it can get dangerous for you. We have the evidence that we need to arrest the couple. Emma has passed it on to Aidan. He and his team are working on verifying it. He thought it would be a couple of days. For now, we need to keep you two away from the couple.”

“And that is hard to do.” Paul sighed, his thoughts troubled as to how to do just that. “We can’t stop living, Abe. If we stay hidden, it would not bring them out.”

“We know that, Paul. Here’s what I suggest.” Richard leaned forward, his elbows resting on his thighs. “Our team has discussed this, argued it over, and come to some plans. We would like to discuss that with you and your team. We’ll work with what you decide to do. We’re here for the duration, Paul. I doubt that it will be long.”

Don was on his feet, heading for the door as he heard the doorbell. He stood where he could observe who was at the door without being seen. He frowned. Now, why was that couple here? They should not be. He stepped backwards and reached for his phone, calling Aidan.

Richard appeared behind him, not sure why Don had not answered the door.

“Don?” His voice was a whisper.

“It’s that couple. Why would they be here?” Don stepped backwards, heading for the office. “We have a situation, people. The couple who we suspect? They're right outside your door now, Paul. I have called Aidan. Is there any reason that they would be here?"

"None." Paul sighed as his head tipped backwards. "Why?"

"That we will leave up to Aidan to find out. I would suspect that it's not for your good." Don pulled out his phone. "Aidan has taken them into custody. He has asked that we remain inside for now. We can still work through what we're planning. Emma?"

"Exactly, Don. This is what we have." Emma went on to detail all that she had found.

Payten stared at her, not sure that what she was hearing was actual fact.

"Emma? What you said about my parents? And the fire?"

"The fire? I have pulled all the reports from then. You were young when it happened and then you disappeared into the foster care system. Your parents' lawyer tried to find you right after it happened. He was in fact your guardian. You should never have been placed in the system. I have his information here. He and his wife are eager to meet you. I have spoken with them.

"In addition to that, I have evidence that the fire was deliberate. It was arson. Someone killed your parents and then made you disappear. How much do you remember of your life with your parents?"

"I know that we never had a lack for anything. Dad was an attorney, working with those who didn't have a lot of money. Mom stayed home." Payten blinked rapidly as tears threatened to overcome her. "Why?"

"Because there is an inheritance that is waiting for you. It is not a huge amount but it is enough to enable you to live comfortably if you're careful. It is to come to you when you're thirty, which is near."

"It is. Who?" Payten felt Paul's arm tighten around her.

"That couple who were here? They're distant cousins to your mother. They decided that the inheritance should come to them. Only, it wouldn't. If you do not claim it by your birthday, it goes into scholarships at the local high school. I have the information that I can give you." Emma suddenly was on her feet, sitting beside Payten, holding her as she sobbed.

Paul nodded and then was on his feet, anger sparking within him. All this over money? He wanted to face that couple and demand from them if a young lady's family had been worth it.

Chapter 44

Aidan appeared in their midst late that afternoon. Not one person had left, not sure if this was over for Paul and Payten. He simply shook his head at Don before he took with gratitude the plate of food that Daci offered him. He had not had a chance to eat at all that day. Aidan listened to the quiet conversation around him, nodding as Abe and Richard sat beside him.

"Aidan? What can we do for you?" Abe's voice was quiet in the noise of conversation around them.

"Pray for Payten and Paul. This is not quite over for them." Aidan stared down at his plate, worry crossing his mind.

Paul and Payten drew back chairs to sit near him, patiently waiting as he ate and then as both Richard and Abe prayed for the situation.

"What can you tell us, Aidan?" Payten spoke at last.

"We have arrested Lewis and Annabelle Todd. They were responsible for the fire that took your parents' lives. They confirmed that they did that and made sure that you went into foster care right away. Money changed hands to have that happen. They were sure that they would receive that inheritance but it was possible. They have watched you over the years and planned on abducting you, forcing you to sign over the inheritance, and then killing you. God had his hand on you, Payten. He protected you in many ways over the years. From what they have told us, they kept a very close eye on you. He is responsible for hiring someone to try and tamper with the evidence that you were working on. This plan came into play when Paul and his team stepped in to protect you. Unfortunately, it was one of the team members in the lab. A recent hire."

Payten started at him before she nodded.

"Of course. He never really fit in. We all questioned his credentials. He never seemed to do much work, although he kept busy."

"That's it exactly, Payten. We have pulled everything that he worked on and sent it over to Riverville as well." Aidan paused to sip at his coffee. "There is someone else, someone that they had been blackmailing."

Paul shared a look with Don and then the rest of their team.

"Judge John Lee." Paul's voice broke through the silence. "That's how they managed to hide Payten in foster care."

"That's correct, Paul. He was arrested this morning in his court office. He became violent with the officers." Aidan didn't say anything else. He didn't need to. They all understood that Judge Lee would not be facing justice on earth.

"I don't know a Judge Lee." Payten was puzzled. She turned to Paul, finding him watching her. "But you did."

"I did, Payten. Our team has had numerous run-ins with him over the years. So has any other security team that has worked in this town." Paul saw Abe and

Richard nodding in agreement. "That's why I was involved. They were desperate to bring both of us down." Paul paused, a thought crossing his mind that maybe it wasn't just them, that someone was after Don. That was something that he would have a long discussion with his team about.

"Anything else?" Aidan looked around at the group, seeing the relief on their faces. "Paul?"

"The bomb? Who set it?"

"No one is admitting to that. We are still investigating that but we have no further information. It is unfortunate that we don't have that person in custody.

Aidan stayed for a while longer before he left. He was exhausted, he decided. *Thank you, Lord, for protecting my friends, for bringing them through this alive. I know that they are closer to You because of this. I just pray for them. I pray for his team. This is not over for them. You are the One who will defend them and protect them. Thank you, Lord, for Your compassion and the peace that only You can give.*

Payten had risen and followed Aidan, watching as he stood for a moment before driving away. She prayed for her friend as she now considered him. A text had come through from Toryn, just stating that he was glad that they had the ones after herself and Paul. It helped. It also helped to have Paul on the road to recovery.

Paul mingled with the people in his house. He was exhausted and should be resting, but he couldn't. He also couldn't completely express his gratitude to the ones who had stepped in. Aileen had been in touch that day, simply asking if she and Samuel could come and spend some time with Payten and himself that weekend. Paul had been grateful to have reconnected with Aileen once more. He didn't know her husband that well but he knew that Samuel would become a friend.

Finding Payten just standing on the front porch, an arm wrapped around a support post, Don gave her a one-armed hug before standing beside her. He didn't speak, letting her be the one who spoke first.

"Thank you, Don. You don't know what this has meant to me." Payten pointed back towards the house.

"I think that I do. You've become part of our family now, Payten. Paul is not letting you walk away. You need each other. God worked through this to bring you two together. Don't lose sight of that."

Payten nodded, her eyes on the stars as they began to twinkle down from the darkening sky. She could hear the sounds of nature as the day and night shifts of critters exchanged places.

"He did, Don. I never expected to find anyone of my own. He knew my dreams and my despairs. I have to now come to terms with what happened to my parents and reach out to the lawyer. It is a shame that he couldn't raise me. I loved him and his wife."

"It is." Don hesitated before he spoke once more. "God was there, Payten, every step of the way. He knew where you needed to be. Who knows what good your work has done over time. Only He knows that. A friend from Abe's team has a saying that goes something like this: God has plans and purposes for our lives that we don't know about."

Payten had turned to watch him, her head nodding as he spoke. She felt Paul's arm around her and leaned back against him.

"That's so true, Don. He wants only the best for us. We can run and hide and walk away from Him. He doesn't move. And He welcomes us back when we return. He does use us in ways that we could not expect or even want to go through. Thank you." Payten reached to hug Don, watching as he walked back into the house.

"Okay, sweetheart?" Paul's voice was low but love-filled.

"I'll get there. And you?"

"I'm okay now that you're safe. We'll digest what we've been told. Aidan will be back with more information over time. Emma will forward what else she has. For now? I'm happy just to be alive with the love of my life in my arms." A kiss was dropped on her cheek, leaving her smiling up at him.

Four months later, Payten turned as Paul approached her, his hand out to reach for hers. He kissed her before wrapping her into a hug. They had been dating now for months, spending as much time as they could together.

Payten had met with the lawyer friend of her father's, Job Cleary. He had simply hugged her and then handed her to his wife, June. They had been devastated when Payten had disappeared and they had not been able to find her.

Payten had accepted what had happened. She grieved for her parents once more but knew that God had protected her over the years. He had also brought Paul into her life and through Paul, his team and Daci. She would be remiss if she didn't thank God each day for their friendship. The five other men on Paul's team considered her a sister, teasing her gently when they were together.

Paul watched his lady love closely. They had taken the time to heal as much as they could. Both had sought out counselling. Gideon had been a great source of support for them both.

"Okay, sweetheart? Where do you want to go today?" Paul grinned down at her.

"The zoo. We have not been back there since we disappeared from there. We know now that the judge was behind that, a threat towards the others. I need to go back there. I need to take back what was taken from us there." She looked up at him, not sure if he would agree.

"I agree totally, sweetheart. It has taken to now for us to do that. I know that Daci and Don have made a number of trips back there. She was ready to do that. You weren't."

"No, neither of us was. We are now." Payten walked out to Paul's truck. She had decided not to rebuild her home, opting instead just to rent a duplex from a couple at their church. She didn't think that she would be on her own for long. Paul had been hinting that way.

Walking through the zoo, Payten's steps slowed as she approached the butterfly building.

"This is it, isn't it, Paul?"

"It is. God is here, sweetheart. He always has been. Take what time that you need." Paul waited patiently for Payten to move, praying for her as she hesitated.

Payten stared at the building, her thoughts muddled for a moment before she moved towards the back of the building. She stared at the wall and then walked away, Paul keeping step with her.

"God was there, wasn't He?" Payten's voice rang with new confidence. "He did protect us and use us to solve things and bring people to justice."

"He did. He does that. I've seen it so much with my friends and their ladies." Paul sat her down on a bench near the river. It had always been a favourite of his as a youth. He bit at his lip, not sure how to proceed. He didn't want to scare Payten away when he spoke and lose the one who completed him.

Payten waited, her eyes on the water. She always found that water relaxed her, the movement of the waves calming. She decided that it was because she knew Who had calmed the storm on the Sea of Galilee. God had calmed many storms within her.

"Payten? I love you. You are the one who completes me. Will you marry me, be mine for life, my partner, my sweetheart?" Paul waited patiently for his lady. He knew that she had to digest what he said before she would respond. If it took hours, days, or weeks for that, he would wait.

Payten blinked rapidly, trying to control her tears. Paul made her feel cherished, loved, wanted, and adored all at once. She nodded, unable to speak.

Paul simply reached to kiss her and then hugged her. He pulled out a ring with a single ruby, slipping it onto her finger. She frowned at the jewel before looking up at him.

"A ruby?"

Paul nodded, knowing that she had not made the connection.

"You are my Proverbs 31 lady, Payten. Your worth to God and to me is far about any precious jewel that man can find on earth.'

Snuggling down in his arms, Payten was content. Paul was as well. God had led them through danger and to one another. It was His plan for their lives.

Thank you for choosing to read the story of Paul and his lady, Payten. His Defenders was not a series that I had ever planned on writing. The six men on the team had other plans. This is Book 1 in the series.

God is our Defender in ways that we can't even begin to comprehend. We need to trust Him in all things. As a human, this is difficult to do. We think that we know best and can run our lives without His help. That never works. We don't know what danger we face every day. My Dad always maintained that God protected us in the simple things. He would use the example of lost keys and having to search for them and simply state that God had allowed us to misplace things to save us from something that we would never know about here on earth. I must say that I have to agree with him. He was a humble man, a carpenter by trade, but he thought deeply about God and His word. His comments would cause our family to think long and hard about how we viewed life and God.

During the writing of this, we underwent the Blizzard of Christmas 2022. I was one of the fortunate ones on the east shore of Lake Erie to not lose my hydro(electricity) even though it did flicker off and back on a few times. I was grateful for a new neighbour, a young man who saw me struggling to shovel the snow and ran across the road with his large scoop and cleared the sidewalks and driveway. At present, I am struggling with excessive damage to a rotator cuff. I trust in God's healing in this as I know that He has allowed this. That was how I was raised.

Now as to the people who walked into the story? This always happens. Abe and his team are in the *His Guardian* series. Abe and Emma are favourite characters of mine. Samuel and Aideen's story is in the *His Warriors* series. Frankie and Deirdre story is *The Storm*, part of *The Haven of Rest* series, one of the earliest ones I wrote. Richard and his team are in the *His Protectors* series. Andrew and Phoebe's story is *The Potter's* Hands. Bill and Cora's story is *Hidden in the* Hollow. I find that my characters rebel and walk back and forth between series. Abe's team is the worst (or best) at doing this, given that Emma has a company that can find anything and anyone no one else can.

Now for the cats? I have two Shelties but I also have two cats. The tuxedo girl is called Ciara (Kira). The little calico is called Caoimhe (Kiva). The animals will find their way into the stories on occasions. Little Caoimhe was born on St. Patrick's Day and of course had to have an Irish name. Both cats have Irish names. A lot of my characters do as well. My maternal side is from Ireland and that heritage just has to come through. As for the others? I name them from the Bible, one way to honour the faith of my Dad.

Once more, thank you for choosing to be part of this new series. I always write my stories with one goal in mind. There is someone out there that needs to hear it, someone that God wants to reach.

God bless each one of you.

Ronna

www.ronnabacon.com

9 781998 821136